Tracking Apache Joe

A small band of renegade Apache led by Broken Hand have captured the daughters of a preacher and are headed for Mexico. After them are Anson Hawkstone and Black Feather, scouting for the army, plus the preacher with four gunmen, and a cavalry patrol that cannot cross the Mexican border.

Added to that, Apache Joe and his Choctaw squaw are trading smallpox and typhoid blankets to Apache villages throughout the territories, and are headed for the village where Hawkstone's woman, Rachel, lives and works as the nurse-doctor.

Closing in on the renegade band, Hawkstone is torn between rescuing the preacher's daughters, and deserting them in a ride to save his woman from disease. Can he do both?

Tracking Apache Joe

George Arthur

A Black Horse Western

ROBERT HALE

© George Arthur 2018
First published in Great Britain 2018

ISBN 978-0-7198-2863-8

The Crowood Press
The Stable Block
Crowood Lane
Ramsbury
Marlborough
Wiltshire SN8 2HR

www.bhwesterns.com

Robert Hale is an imprint
of The Crowood Press

Typeset by
Derek Doyle & Associates, Shaw Heath
Printed and bound in Great Britain by
4Bind Ltd, Stevenage, SG1 2XT

ONE

Five Apache warriors with painted faces and no shirts jumped Anson Hawkstone when he reached the final bluff coming down from the woods. They rode at him, two from the right, three from the left, sitting high, rifles at their shoulders, still a hundred yards out. Mesquite dripped with recent 1876 April rain. When Hawkstone reached the plain, he heeled the chestnut to a gallop. She jumped ahead, her eight-year-old legs eager to run. He pulled the Winchester. He didn't know if these Mescalero were part of the band who took the preacher's daughters, or they broke away from Geronimo, or they were just an ornery bunch after his rifle and cartridges and horse. The two on the right were closest. They both fired, the slugs chewed damp sand at the chestnut's pounding hoofs. Hawkstone stood stiff in the stirrups, twisted around, and brought the Winchester to his shoulder. He timed his position to the gallop of the chestnut and fired. His first shot had a warrior bouncing off his pony. The crack of rifle fire became lost along the plain. Hawkstone swung the rifle across. He fired and ejected three times. Only one brave was knocked off the rump of his mount.

They were closing to fifty yards but the young chestnut started to outdistance them. Hawkstone kept his knees pushed against the saddle, making his body rock with the mare's stretching legs as she ran. The three Apache fell in behind and rode pursuit. Hawkstone returned the Winchester to its scabbard. It required two hands to fire and eject. He pulled his Colt .45 Peacemaker. Open desert air cracked with Apache rifle shots. Hawkstone didn't want the chestnut at full speed, she'd wear herself down. The Apache ponies already began to slow, the pace too fast too long. A bullet zinged a crease across Hawkstone's left stirrup. Horses running spoiled any decent aim. Hawkstone swung his arm back and straight out. He fired, cocked, fired – a brave hunched forward. His arms wrapped around his pony's neck. He slowed. One rider slowed with him. He went alongside and helped his wounded companion stay mounted as the pony eased to a stop. The third rider kept coming, but slower. Hawkstone gently pulled reins to slow the chestnut. As she bounced to a trot, he turned her around to face the warrior riding hard for him, and stopped her. He holstered the Colt and pulled the Winchester again. He reckoned they were empty or about to be. He raised the rifle to his shoulder and watched the Apache sit tall, rein in, and stop.

The chestnut panted under Hawkstone, standing on damp desert sand, her sides pushed in and out against stirrups. About twenty yards away the Apache sat, his rifle across the saddle. His pony heaved heavily, its belly and sides puffing with each breath. The warrior stared, his passive painted face waited, waiting for the killing bullet. Behind him, the two others had dismounted, one helped the other with his wound. Hawkstone lowered the rifle. He relaxed in the saddle. He and the brave sat their heavy-breathing horses and stared at each other. Hawkstone shoved the Winchester back in its scabbard. The chestnut's breathing began to slow. Still, he sat and the Apache sat, looking across a small patch of Arizona territory sand and mesquite and fresh growing spring flowers at each other.

They might have been from the band he was dogging, Broken Hand and Small Dog who jumped the reservation and possibly headed for Geronimo at the Canyon de los Embudos in Mexico to show off their captives. It was Broken Hand and his band of fifteen who took the Baptist preacher Isaac Dawson's daughters, Laura Jean, eighteen; Edna, seventeen; Lucille, sixteen. These face-painted Mescalero braves in front of him weren't from Broken Hand. They likely broke away from Geronimo, to get distance from the renegade Apache who attracted too much gunfire and heat, and was probably as crazy as a loco-weed-eating mustang.

Hawkstone moved his gaze from the man sitting mounted in front of him to the pair behind. One pushed up from the ground, keeping the cloth pushed against the wound of his companion. The wounded man was helped to the back of his pinto. Hawkstone looked closer at the mounted Apache opposite him. What he saw were men, men just like him – not big or fat or greedy men, but thin small hungry men – trying to make their way in life while others that owned everything, and wanted everything schemed to take that way of life away. He felt no hatred for the Apache. He only shot at these fellas because they were shooting at him.

The two horses stood facing each other twenty yards apart, breathing deeply but no longer panting. Hawkstone kept both hands on the saddle horn. He raised his right arm high, stiff, fingers pointed to a milky blue sky.

The warrior raised his arm. They sat on their horses with arms raised for a half a minute. Hawkstone silently watched and waited.

The Apache dropped his arm. He turned his pony and walked it back toward his two fellow riders.

Hawkstone reined the chestnut around and trotted off to cross the road to Tucson, on his way to Rachel.

A patrol of ten cavalry soldiers waited for Hawkstone on the road five miles northwest of Tucson. Four were mounted, two on each side of the road. Six others lounged around a 10 x square tent, their horses picketed behind. They watched Hawkstone ride west along the trail, keeping the chestnut at an easy walk. As he approached, the lounging soldiers stood. The four on horseback closed to a line blocking his way. Hawkstone reined in.

An officer emerged from the tent, a captain in his late twenties. His uniform showed smart, and jangled excess equipment for the warming weather. He looked up at Hawkstone with serious blue eyes. 'Good afternoon, sir. Captain Milton Ferguson. You will please dismount.'

'What for?'

Captain Ferguson made it obvious he did not like looking up at Hawkstone. The four mounted boys edged closer. Hawkstone couldn't think of them as men. Pour milk on their face and a cat might lick off any whiskers. No need to slip the rawhide thong off his Colt. With eleven of them he'd be cut down before he dropped more than one or two. He wasn't going to war with the cavalry, even if they were blue-belly Yankees.

The captain said, 'Please, sir, I'd rather we talk in the relative comfort of the tent. We heard gunshots and were about to investigate when we saw you riding in.'

Hawkstone swung down from the saddle. One of the standing uniform boys took the reins. A grizzled, whiskey-faced sergeant opened the tent flap, the only elder in uniform. Inside the tent was a table, a cot and three camp chairs. A ledger sat on the table. The captain was small but he and Hawkstone crowded the space. Hawkstone removed his plains hat and combed his fingers through his hair.

Captain Ferguson blinked, looking up at Hawkstone's hazel eyes. 'You're a big one all right. What are you, six six?'

'More like six four and 200.'

'That curly light hair makes you look like a Viking. You got that kind of ancestry?'

'Mebbe. Why you got me in this tent?' The captain looked like he should stay out of stiff winds or he'd blow to the horizon.

The sergeant stood at the flap opening. 'Nothing else, sir?'

Hawkstone said, 'No tents for the troops?'

That drew a smile from the sergeant who didn't wait for an answer, but closed the flap as he left.

Captain Ferguson removed his hat to show straight light hair like the late General Custer. He took off a sword belt and tossed it and the hat on the cot. He waved to a folding canvas chair and sat on the one opposite across the table. A lantern glowed between them.

'We are not here for the night. We'll be off on night patrol shortly.' He opened the ledger. 'What is your name, sir?'

'Anson Hawkstone.'

He wrote that in the ledger. He looked up with a frown. 'Where you headed?'

'Northwest. Toward the San Pedro River. A small village a day out of Fort McLane where I live.'

'You live with Apache?'

'I live with Rachel, the medicine woman. I'll be visiting a day or two then rid south to the border.' Hawkstone hadn't seen Rachel in a month.

The captain brushed the top of the ledger of dust. 'There's a scout working out of Fort Lowell by the name of Hawkstone. That be you?'

'Temporary. I'm helping them locate the preacher's daughters taken by a band of Mescalero. Army scouts seen them headed through Apache Pass. The preacher and a gang of four gunslingers had chased them toward Fort Lowell. He convinced the army to take up interest. They might be headed for Texas now.'

'Wasn't Geronimo. He jumped the reservation again. Hear he's already deep in Mexico.'

'And you boys cut back on food for his people . . .

10

again. No, this is a small band of renegades mebbe looking for some sport. Broken Hand, Small Dog, and their bands. About seventeen all told.'

Ferguson sat quiet in his own thoughts for a spell, his gaze on the page of the ledger. He looked back up at Hawkstone with his baby blue eyes and clean schoolboy face. 'Are you aware Apache Joe and his squaw are in the area?'

Hawkstone leaned back, his eyes wide. 'You don't say. I figured they was in Mexico for life. No need for his brand of blanket trader in the territories.'

'They spread smallpox and typhoid with their trade, wipe out villages and take more infected blankets.'

Hawkstone nodded. 'They got to be removed from living.'

The captain closed the ledger and squinted. 'You were confronted by Apache just now?'

'Confronted? Don't know nothing about confronted. Five war-painted braves jumped me when I come off the bluff. I didn't know them. None was Apache Joe.'

'Did you kill them?'

'Two of 'em.'

'And the other three?'

Hawkstone sat straight on the chair. It was uncomfortable and he wanted to be back outside, on his way. 'We sort of made an unspoken truce. I figured they was out of cartridges. One I shot was wounded pretty good.'

'Were you also out of cartridges?'

'Nope, I had a few shots left.'

The captain frowned. 'Empty? And you didn't pursue them?'

'They was done.'

'But you could have finished them off.'

'Had no reason to.'

'Mr Hawkstone, you are a scout. You are aware the Apache conduct raids all over the territory? The hostiles are killing and scalping people – women and children, helpless settlers. And with Apache Joe roaming the territories. . . .'

'Mebbe so, mebbe not so much as folks make out. It's got nothing to do with me. Me and them braves had a tussle together and we set up a truce without talking, and I went on my way.'

'But they will live to kill again.'

'Probably.'

'But . . . you should have finished them. You should have killed them all. It's your duty.'

Hawkstone glared at him. 'It ain't my duty, soldier boy. I ain't in the cavalry. It's up to you yellow-leg-stripe army boys to go on out there and slaughter Apache men, women, children – horses and dogs, – kittens and puppies.'

TWO

Rachel Cleary, Good Squaw, the medicine woman, gathered Hawkstone into her arms and held him close to her breasts. He knew he took too much time with her. But he had been away a month, and going after the renegade band, he didn't know how much longer they would be apart. It might be another month, or more. They lay on her bed inside the hut, the hut where she spent her days nursing sick and wounded villagers. Darkness was total for the moon had not yet risen. Coyotes yelped at each other down by the river.

'How early do you leave?' she asked.

'Sunrise. You got to be careful, woman. I hear Apache Joe and his squaw are in the territories.'

'I've heard of them. Don't they spread disease?'

'Blanket and hide traders. Spread typhoid and smallpox. They can wipe out a band or village in weeks.'

'I'll warn the village.' She pushed closer to him. 'How long will you be away?'

'The band is a day ahead. I figure the girls will slow them some. I can catch them this side or down Mexico way, don't matter.'

'The cavalry can't cross the border,' she said.

'If they ain't already across, mebbe I can slow them on this side until the army gets there.' He felt her breath against his throat. 'I don't want to be gone more'n a month or so.'

'Those three girls,' she said. 'What they must be going through.'

He kissed her forehead. 'You been through it. You know.'

'Yes, I know. If you rescue the girls, won't the army want you to keep after Geronimo?'

'They will. But it won't do them no good.'

'He's jumped the reservation before.'

'And will again. Newspaper reporters like him on account of he's so entertaining. Nobody talks or writes about the harm he does to his people with his fooling around.'

Rachel smiled at him. 'You don't like the Apache outlaw much, do you?'

'He oughta be shot dead. Dead on sight.'

They were silent for a spell. She kissed his throat. 'I'm thinking on Ben's letter.'

'You sure you want to change your life? Be that close to me all the time?'

'Lately, you've been gone from me too long. Yes, I want us closer, close together. If it means sharing a ship cabin while crossing oceans, I ain't saying no.'

'You might take a liking to it.'

'Just so we're together.' She wore nothing and she wiggled next to him. 'I'll miss Little Rain, and mostly the children, but I'm ready for change.' She moved her head down from his throat and rubbed her nose with her finger against the tickle of his chest hair. 'I wish Black Feather was back from Mexico. Little Rain still pines for him.'

'I pine for you, woman.'

'No need. You only have to be here to get everything a man would want.' She lifted the thick hair curls to look at his face. 'You know that.'

'Yes'm, I do. I'll get back soon as I can.'

'But we're together now.'

'Yes'm.' He enjoyed his hands on her.

'I don't want you weary on the trail come morning.'

'I won't mind,' he said.

In the morning, the dawn wet, low prairie animals on the prowl, the village beginning to stir, Rachel and Hawkstone stood outside her hut. She kept touching him, as if refusing to let him go. He saddled the chestnut mare. She gave him a package of antelope jerky and biscuits for the early part of the trail. With the food in his saddle bags, he saw Little Rain approach, long-legged and lean, dark eyes shiny, wearing her deerskin dress with calf-high moccasins, her seventeen-year-old oval face just a little sour from fresh sleep.

Without hesitation, Little Rain wrapped her arms around Hawkstone and on her tip toes kissed the side of his neck. 'You leave again?'

'Help Rachel warn the village. Apache Joe prowls the territory.'

Little Rain stood back with a frown. 'I know of Apache Joe and Tattoo.'

'Once I take care of this army business, I'll be tracking the pair of them.'

'You put an end to them, Hawkstone.'

'That's my intent, little girl.'

'We have braves who will help you.'

'They'd be welcome.'

They stood uneasy because there were three of them and Hawkstone wanted his farewell to Rachel to be private. As if sensing they wanted to be alone, Little Rain went in the hut and closed the curtain.

Rachel wrapped her arms around Hawkstone's neck and kissed him long and wet. He caressed her and clutched her close to him with his face buried in her sweet-smelling red hair. Beyond a reasonable time to let her go, he kept holding her. She felt good and smelled good and gave him warm memories of their lovemaking. She remained still in his arms. He continued to hold her tight, unable to release her, and he did not know why.

'I love you with every part of me,' she whispered.

'I do want a life at sea again,' he said, 'but only if, when I reach out I touch you. You are the love of my life and that's a fact.'

'Hurry home to me.' She pushed back with a smile. 'Now, you leave me with a Ben Franklyn, my love.'

Hawkstone stood with the reins in his hand. He looked out toward sunrise while his mind flowed to remember. He smiled down at her. '*A man without a woman and firelight, is like a body without soul or spirit.*'

'Your woman will be waiting,' she said as he mounted.

He looked back as the chestnut walked away, and saw smoke from the scattered teepees of the village. She stood in front of the hut, a misty rising sun making her glow.

THREE

The first day, he rode easy to get Rachel off his mind and skin, so he might concentrate on the task at hand. She crowded his thoughts and he had to let that ease before he began the quick pursuit. As the day progressed, he reckoned he was not alone. His first night on the trail, Hawkstone was sure he had company. As he unsaddled and set up his camp next to a juniper, he kept the rawhide loop off the hammer of his Colt. He had caught signs of a rider all day, not a complete sight but glimpses, a shadow, a puff of dirt kicked up by horse hoofs, a silhouette against tan hills. His company was a single rider, Apache, but he wasn't sure who.

After he ground coffee beans and had Arbuckle coffee boiling, he squatted close to the fire and pretended to stare into it while his glance darted at the darkness around. When he heard moccasins grind sand in a sliding step, he stood and pulled the Colt and cocked the hammer.

'Step into the campfire light, or I'll drop you. You won't get no more warning.'

Moving Rock cleared his throat and shuffled forward enough to be seen. 'Hawkstone,' he said. 'You remember me. I am Moving Rock. I make you well when bandits cut you down.'

'Yes.' Hawkstone holstered the Colt. 'You're too old and crippled to be wandering out here in the dark. Why you trailing me?'

The old Apache came closer to the fire. There was not enough light to see him completely but Hawkstone remembered. He was sixty or so, in filthy buckskin, firelight making his wide head scar shine. He had once been scalped by a warrior from another nation, but the warrior had been young and the cutting sloppy, so Moving Rock made enough time to shove a knife through the young heart. He had a large hook nose, and another thin knife scar across his throat. The old warrior had lived through many events. Without front teeth he was mostly silent. When stagecoach bandits shot up Hawkstone and he rode off a cliff into the river in escape, and barely made it to the opposite shore, it had been Moving Rock who used some kind of putrid herbal mud patches to start the healing process. Then he built a travois to reunite Hawkstone with his long-ago love, Rachel Cleary, the medicine woman.

Moving Rock squatted by the fire. He put his gnarled hands out and rubbed them together. 'Old bones can't get warm.' He took the cup of coffee Hawkstone offered and had a shallow sip. 'Good,' he said. 'Hawkstone make decent coffee. Not as good as some women of the village, or Rachel the medicine woman, but good enough to drink.'

Hawkstone smiled. 'Wasn't expecting company.'

That brought a grunt from Moving Rock. 'You track Apache Joe?'

Hawkstone squatted next to the old warrior and sipped. 'Not jest yet.'

'You go to rescue captured girls, then.'

'If I can catch Broken Hand's band. I understand the girl's preacher pa got hisself four gunslingers ahead of me. And a lieutenant's bringing up the rear with a patrol.'

Moving Rock nodded. He sipped and looked at Hawkstone over the rim of the tin cup. 'Geronimo?'

'He ain't in my pocket of interest. He'll do what he does and I ain't got nothing to do with that.'

Moving Rock moved to sit with his legs crossed. He held the coffee cup in both hands and stared into it. 'You better track Apache Joe.'

'I told you, I will. A detachment out of Fort McLane is dogging him now.'

'The San Pedro toward the Rio Gila – he cross those rivers, he doubles around, no detachment good. You track Apache Joe, Hawkstone.'

'I'm on the army payroll the rest of the month. I got to go after them girls first.'

'Be quick then, do not be too long. Do not be late.'

Hawkstone tossed grounds out of his cup, thinking. The old Apache kept his conscience nagging at him. He knew what he should be doing, but he had a contract, obligations.

'Them cavalry boys will keep him running. He won't have time to stop and trade. The village has been warned.'

'The cavalry will try to arrest him and they will all die. You are the one.'

'I'll get to him. No telling what is happening to them girls. They can't be abandoned. What if their pa can't find them? The patrol is even farther behind and it can't cross to Mexico. You want to ride south with me? Think that swayback pinto can keep up?'

Moving Rock emptied his cup. He leveled a stare at Hawkstone, then nodded toward the juniper. 'I sleep there, now. I stay close to village.' He pointed a crooked finger at Hawkstone. 'Do not linger with pretty girls. Be quick with Broken Hand. You must track Apache Joe. You must run him down and kill him, and burn him to cinders, him and that Choctaw squaw of his and the horses and blankets and hides. Do not be late, Hawkstone. Do not be late.'

Anson Hawkstone rode his chestnut hard and fast, from a gallop to canter, then rested with plenty of water for the mare, then mounted, heeling her on. The flowers around the trail bloomed from heavy early April rain. Flowers in rainbow colors spread around and in front of him, his ignorance of such things did not allow him to identify. Their sweet fresh smell filled his nostrils as his mount galloped beneath him. He knew he could not linger at Fort Thomas. Hawkstone had to head farther southwest to Fort Lowell. That was where the lieutenant's patrol left from to pursue Broken Hand. He had no idea where the preacher and his gunmen were. Maybe still in Fort Thomas. Maybe after the renegades, in front of the patrol.

Hawkstone had to somehow pass them both.

He saw the adobe fort long before he reached it. He didn't want to stop, but he needed information. Two days of hard riding left him aching and weary. He and the chestnut needed a day of rest but he did not want to be inside the fort too long. Fort Thomas carried a history of sickness and disease.

Recently, malaria had spread through the fort. The source had been a popular well soldiers and families drew water from. Though the well had been filled and closed, traces of the disease lingered. At times it went away, but there were other sources, other pools of still water, where mosquitoes bred, and the disease always seemed to come back. Hawkstone intended to stay outside – no eating, drinking or sleeping inside the adobe walls. Those east coast newspapers might have been right about the West, what with malaria, and poor hygiene, and blanket traders like Apache Joe spreading typhoid and smallpox about. More folks in the West died of disease than gunshots, though many an eager, wanna be gunslinger expired from self-inflicted gunshot wounds while practising the draw.

Approaching the fort at sunset, Hawkstone saw tepees outside the wall. He slowed the chestnut to a walk. He reached down and patted the side of her neck. She was a good mount – a man could not ask for better. Through smoke from the tepees, a cavalry patrol moved to the fort slow and tired clanging through the open fort gates, the men with heads bent, bodies slack, shadows in the coming darkness. Hawkstone did not permit himself to wonder where they came from. He was tired himself and just wanted a small spot of land to spread his saddle and blanket. Some Arbuckle coffee, a chunk of the antelope jerky Rachel had given him, maybe a handful of oats for the chestnut and he was done for the night. Any questions he had could wait until morning.

He found a spot just beyond the tepees along the top of a small bluff. Listening to muffled voices from those outside the fort, he was drinking the final cup of coffee, ready to stretch out next to the fire when he felt, rather than saw, somebody approach.

'Hawkstone,' a soft voice said as a man approached.

Hawkstone already had his Colt in his hand. 'Show yourself with empty hands and step close to the fire.'

When he saw his Apache blood brother, he relaxed and eased the hammer of his weapon. 'Black Feather,' he said. He holstered the Colt and gripped the young man's upper arms with a grin. 'You are back from Mexico.'

FOUR

Done with his nightly prayer, Isaac Dawson leaned back against his saddle away from the campfire. Of the four men riding with him, Magruder snored loudly. Gowie and Hoback talked softly on the other side of the flame. Iron Shirt, their scout, was away seeking the location of Broken Hand and the girls. Two days out of Fort Lowell and the army patrol was still a day behind. But they also had scouts.

And all of them were going in the wrong direction.

Why would Broken Hand head east toward Fort Bowie and back to New Mexico Territory? Did he intend to cross Texas for the Mexican border? The savage had to be riding for Mexico. He knew the cavalry could not follow. Nothing would stop Isaac Dawson from crossing the border and rescuing his daughters. But that would be after Broken Hand and Small Dog and all fifteen savages riding with them had met the Lord's sweet justice – the wrath of God brought down on them by the four gunmen riding with Isaac. The gunmen were ungodly to be sure, but they were merely instruments doing God's business as directed by Isaac Dawson, the preacher in God's church dictating His command.

Isaac Dawson had wanted his church in Albuquerque, a civilized city in sad need of being saved. Like most of the southwest, Catholic missions were dominated by heavy Mexican manipulation. Ornate missions and churches influenced by the architects of Spain appeared to be on every street corner of every town and city. Isaac had seen himself with a large congregation of followers, drawn to a faith that allowed them to be reborn in the light of Jesus, allowed their souls to be saved. There were no priests proclaiming to be direct representatives of the Lord, but a man as they were men, explaining the word of God, a man ordained in St. Louis as a Baptist minister. True, his parents had told him he must be of good character because as a man, tall, skinny, with a big nose and dark eyes close together, he carried little in looks that might be called attractive. He kept himself clean-shaven and always wore a formal blue suit with his shoes brightly polished. He knew he was ugly, he didn't need his parents to constantly remind him.

Isaac stared into the fire, listening to the gargle sounds from Magruder. No, he as a young ambitious servant of the Lord would not have his church in Albuquerque. He was sent to Valencia, many miles south, where he carried on the white man's burden, bringing the word of God to heathen and white ignorant alike. Bitter as a single man, he soon paired himself with a Shoshone princess moving with a small band headed north. Though he had personally performed his own marriage ceremony, guilt plagued his so-called married life because he was, in fact, living in sin with the woman, and he knew it. She bore him three daughters then died of typhoid fever. He was left with raising the girls himself, a just punishment for his sinful coupling. And sinful it was, his thoughts of her always wicked, full of lust and desire and physical pleasure, having his fill of her yet wanting more.

Now those thoughts came back to assault him.

The girls, two carrying the beauty of their mother, had grown to a dangerous age.

Laura Jean, the oldest at eighteen, most resembled her mother – tall, long-legged, slender, tawny skin, dark eyes, long black hair, easy movement – Isaac often had to force himself to look away from her. Though a half-breed, Laura Jean appeared and moved too much as her mother had, in innocence yet seductive, her glide and sway and stretch inborn and sensuous, out of her control. She drew the gaze and stare of men, and had since she was fourteen. She wanted to be a school teacher and was training at the Apache reservation. Isaac discouraged her from talking too much with boys, especially the savages. But the brave, Broken Hand, kept slipping around, waiting outside the school house, looking at her in that certain way. To Isaac, it was obvious what the animal wanted. By dumb luck the other two girls, Lucille and Edna were walking with Laura Jean when Broken Hand kidnapped her. All three were taken by Broken Hand, his little friend, Small Dog and fifteen young bucks. They all wanted the same thing, and now they had all three girls.

Lucille, the youngest daughter at sixteen, was the wildest of the three. Small in stature, unlike her parents, she was openly proud of her tiny body, and at sixteen, boldly flirted and teased neighboring boys – and even older men. She had a pretty, petulant face and the blonde hair of her father which she wore long in ringlets. She constantly worked to pull attention from her older sister. More troubling for Isaac, Lucille appeared to hate the restriction of a religious pious life. She was rebellious and often skipped church services to picnic with boys – and he suspected, to swim with them in the river, possibly without clothes. Whipping her to repent her sinful ways did no good. It brought perhaps one day of obedience, then more, deeper rebellion.

Of his three daughters, Isaac Dawson only had Edna, his middle girl at seventeen, as an ally on the pathway to the Lord. Unfortunately, Edna looked much more like her father than her mother – the same nose, dark eyes, but not the gangly frame. Her red cheeks were chubby and the rest of her followed the same way. She ignored boys and their shouted names and those who called her fat. When she spoke, which was seldom, it was to praise the glory of Jesus, and dedication to her father. It was Edna who silently helped prepare for the church services, and weekly meetings for Bible study. She taught Sunday School and conducted youth group prayers. Isaac had to admit, though he needed all three of his daughters returned, it was Edna he missed most.

Isaac stirred when he heard Iron Shirt ride back into camp. Gowie and Hoback grunted a greeting. Even Magruder coughed in his sleep.

Cross-eyed Gowie said, 'We got some red-eye. You look like you could use a snort.'

The Apache, Iron Shirt, tied his snorting black stallion to the string and stepped into the camp and took the offered bottle. He pulled hard from it and coughed and handed it back.

'Tell you boys right off. They're young. Fifteen of them will be hard to kill. Where's the preacher?' He looked across the fire. 'Yeah.'

'You saw them?' Isaac asked.

'No, I didn't. But a fella I know did, about two days ago.' Though Iron Shirt came from the Mescalero tribe, he had told Isaac that he adapted to white man's ways because the white man lived a lot better than Apache. Others of his tribe had better do the same or they were headed for oblivion. He squatted next to Isaac and blew his nose into the fire holding one nostril at a time, without any cloth.

'They circled around. Drew the patrol out of Apache Pass toward Fort Bowie, and now did a turn-around and best I can figure they is headed directly toward Skeleton Canyon.'

'And Mexico,' Isaac said.

'Yup, and Mexico.'

Gowie and Hoback had gone back to their whiskey and low conversation. Isaac stared at Iron Shirt with tight lips. 'We can get in front of the patrol.'

'Yes, sir. Mebbe, if we ride hard enough we can catch them in the canyon, before they reach the border.'

'We might set up an ambush.'

'That'd be a stretch, get in front of them.'

The word 'ambush' had Gowie's and Hoback's attention. They moved around the fire toward Isaac and squatted to the creak of their holster leather.

Gowie said, 'You figure to just cut them down, Mr Dawson?'

Isaac looked from on to the other – Gowie, cross-eye and partially scalped (he tried to hide the scar with a woollen watch cap) – and Hoback, shorter than the others and wearing a Montana Peak hat.

Isaac's deceased woman, the mother of his three girls, had come to him with what she called her dowry, a leather pouch filled with gold nuggets. From time to-time he questioned her on how she acquired the nuggets and where they came from. She never told him. Through the years they had needed a nugget or two, but the pouch was still half-filled when she died. Isaac had used the nuggets to hire these gunmen.

He said, 'Gentlemen, though you are non-believers, we are the instruments of God's wrath. We ride with purpose. We will smite these heathens and take back my girls. No way to know what those animals have been doing to my innocent children, but they will all die in the name of the Lord.'

Iron Shirt nodded. 'Yes, sir. Whatever kind of name we shoot 'em down in, we better get riding on account of we got us another element.'

From the shadows on the other side of the campfire, Magruder said, 'The scout from Fort McLane, or Fort Lowell, or mebbe even Fort Thomas.'

Isaac rubbed his mouth. 'What about him?'

Iron Shirt shifted position. 'He ain't at Fort Thomas no more. He's ahead of us. Ahead of us and ahead of them soldiers, tracking down that band of hostiles.'

Isaac looked from one to the other. 'So, who is this scout?'

Iron Shirt stared at Isaac. 'His name is Hawkstone. Only he ain't alone no more. He's got a friend, an Apache – actually his blood brother – Black Feather, mebbe the best tracker in the whole southwest.'

FIVE

Late afternoon, as Hawkstone swung down from the chestnut, Black Feather used his moccasin to push cold ashes.

'How long you figure,' Hawkstone asked, 'a day, mebbe less?'

Black Feather widened his walk around the ashes. He looked the same before he went to Mexico, when they both lived with the annihilation of their small village by the cavalry and the death of those close to them. He was in his twenties, six feet, wore buckskin, had straight black hair to his shoulders, handsome enough to likely still be wanted by maidens and non-maidens alike, and he indulged a few. At the edge of the clearing, he pushed through thick mesquite.

'Wild pig leavings, they dressed and sectioned here.' He spoke Chiricahua with the southwest dialect which he sometimes slipped into. Hawkstone grew up with the Apache and identified the meaning of the words, and at times – when they didn't want others to know – they spoke Apache. Though Hawkstone knew Chiricahua, he could not wrap his head around the different dialects, different depending on the area, not to mention the language of other tribes – Sioux, Pawnee, Navaho, Cherokee, Choctaw, and so many others, each with different dialects. Some he might understand if similar, but by now in the years of history, he figured most Indians understood some English. Even Indian tribes did not understand the dialects of other tribes. English became the common language of the land, brought by European invaders who expanded west with wagons and railroads to roll over and destroy tepees in their path. He and Black Feather usually talked English, but sometimes Black Feather glided into his native tongue, and Hawkstone would reply in like.

Hawkstone walked beyond the campsite to the track of horses. 'They took off at a gallop. They spent part of the night and rode out fast.'

Black Feather looked off in the direction the band went. 'The girls ride their own ponies. They leave their sweet smell behind.'

Even Hawkstone could smell the girls. He looked around the clearing, then at Black Feather. 'Did they do anything here? I see the men, and mebbe where the girls sat huddled together. I don't see where they did anything to the girls.'

Black Feather stepped to a clump of smooth bounders. 'Girls sit here. One man, Broken Hand, with the big moccasin feet, stand close. They eat some roasted pig here. They eat and maybe talk.' He turned back to Hawkstone. 'No, girls not touched here. But. . . .'

'What is it?'

Black Feather walked to a juniper and studied the ground around it. 'Broken Hand sit here. One of the girls sit next to him.'

'Which one?'

Black Feather shrugged. 'I am just an Apache. I cannot know everything.'

Hawkstone squinted. 'So you say. You figure one of the girls pushed off that rock over there and came to sit next to Broken Hand?'

Black Feather smiled. 'It is good to be riding again with my blood brother. I missed the talk, the questions – the creaky way you move.'

'Forties ain't that old.'

'You are getting along in years. You better get back to Rachel, and soon.'

Hawkstone pointed a finger at him. 'Don't you start with me. I already got my conscience clawing at me from Moving Rock. I know Apache Joe is out there. We'll get to tracking him after we rescue them little girls. I got a contract with the army.'

Black Feather looked away. 'A contract.'

'I got to finish what I started. I ride for the brand. I put my name on a piece of paper, scratched it out plain.'

'Then I go after Apache Joe.'

'This rescue goes faster if we're together. We got gunmen, a fanatical preacher, and the United States Cavalry breathing down our back. You know Little Dog.'

'Not well.'

'And you don't like him.'

'He has a woman fat with child in a village. He knows Apache Joe roams the area. Yet, he drinks whiskey with

33

his boyhood hunting friend and goes on a kidnap raid. Three young white girls. What did he think would happen with their preacher pa?'

'Many men grow old without growing up,' Hawkstone said.

'Is that a Ben Franklyn?'

'I don't think so, but it'll do.'

Black Feather stepped to his pinto. 'They are six to eight hours in front. We better get riding before the gunmen catch up to us.'

Next morning, at Devil's Kitchen, the entrance to Skeleton Canyon, flanked by flat mesa where jagged steeple rocks stood twice as high as a man on horseback, the party had stopped again. Ground was flat and craggy, the canyon bordering the Peloncillo Mountains along the New Mexico Territory border, not dry enough for dust. A carpet of flowers spread in all directions, surrounding green mesquite, with several streams. Air was clear and cool. Hawkstone figured they were close enough to see dust if it was there. The band stopped often, no doubt due to the girls. The pace of the trail had to be hard on them. If Hawkstone and Black Feather drew close, so might others.

It was obvious, Broken Hand rode for the border. Once across into Mexico he would not be concerned about the cavalry. But the preacher would keep coming, border or no. Broken Hand must have been concerned about the four gunmen, as Hawkstone was. If the girls were being violated, there would be killing, the preacher would see to that. Hawkstone had not met any of them, not the girls, Broken Hand, Small Dog, the preacher, the four gunmen, nor even the lieutenant in charge of the cavalry patrol. During a brief stop at Fort Lowell he had learned Lieutenant Edgar Wilson was barely over twenty and fresh from riding a desk. He had ten soldiers with him, most young, from training back East. Forts and camps were being built all over the southwest and an avalanche of fresh army recruits had been sent West to occupy them. They joined an occasional Civil War veteran who was either a drunk, or a sergeant, or both. The government was determined to deal with the Indian problem by throwing money, ammunition and school-boy-faced young men at it. To Hawkstone, it meant the end of a wandering free way of life he and men like him had once known. All western living creatures from animals to men now saw changes in their lives. Nobody would ever be the same again. Hawkstone reckoned the changes must be good for some folks, just not anyone he knew.

'Hawkstone,' Black Feather said. 'You ride quiet. Your face is twisted in thought.' The horses walked, resting between gallops.

Hawkstone looked to the east, beyond his blood brother toward the mountains and New Mexico Territory. 'Broken Hand sends a rider back to watch us. He stays in the hills.'

'Yes. I have seen him.'

Hawkstone twisted in his saddle to look back. 'Another rider dogs us.'

'Iron Shirt. He rides with the preacher.'

'You know him?'

'I know of him. He is quick on the draw, like the other three.'

Hawkstone sat stiff in the saddle. 'This ain't getting no better for us, brother. We're likely to get caught in a sandwich.'

Black Feather nodded. 'It will be worse if Broken Hand decides to turn and hide so he can dry-gulch us.'

'That might let the preacher and soldiers catch up.'

'It will give him time to rest his horses before a hard push to the border.'

Hawkstone squinted ahead, trying to see movement. 'We all got to rest these horses. Unsaddle them and rub them down. Give them feed and water. We're wearing them out.'

Feather reached down and patted his pinto's neck. 'I will ride fast ahead – let Small Dog know I come in peace, and you want to talk with Broken Hand. We can see how things are, if the girls are being violated. I will carry a white flag.'

Hawkstone nodded. 'Think I'll circle back and check on them gunmen, mebbe meet the preacher pa, catch the make of him, see if I can slow them some.'

'Be mindful of Iron Shirt. He is watching.'

'I know.'

'He is a back shooter, Hawkstone. He will wait until you turn away.'

'Then he'll always see my front,' Hawkstone said.

SIX

Riding at a gallop, Isaac Dawson still carried his Bible. The times they slowed, he opened it to any random place and began to read. Interesting to him, he also carried an Army Colt at his side. It was there to deal out justice for the Lord. He bounced in the saddle as the gelding eased to a fast trot, then walked his mount like the three riders around him. He barely saw the entrance to Skeleton Canyon ahead. It shimmered in afternoon sunlight. He sweated in his blue suit.

Hoback, wearing his once white – now gray – Montana Peak hat, with sweat stains around the band, spoke first. 'We better get off and walk a spell, get the weight off their backs.'

'You say there is water ahead?' Isaac asked.

Hoback pulled off his hat and wiped the inside with his filthy shirt tail. 'With all the rain there should be plenty. Dry creeks and rivers filling. In another couple months it'll all be dry again. Got to be careful of still ponds though, there are mosquitoes and still some malaria around.' He replaced his hat.

Cross-eyed Gowie with the scalp scar showing from

the front of the wool watch cap was the first to dismount. He took a long pull from his canteen. 'Them soldier boys got to be two days or more behind.'

Magruder swung down behind and hawked a wad of green spit to the side. 'With fresher horses they ain't wearing down. Mr Dawson, why you want us to catch them two scouts?'

Walking beside his gelding, Isaac didn't want to tell these gunmen he had checked on the scouts, only to learn as Iron Shirt confirmed, the scout Black Feather was the best tracker in the southwest. His companion, Hawkstone, was almost as good. Both were much better at tracking than Iron Shirt, the man more white than Apache. Isaac wanted the scouts working for him. He needed to know the trail and where along the border the band would cross – and he had enough gold nuggets left to entice them. A story told at Fort Lowell had it that since Black Feather was the best, the army wanted him working for them. According to the major, why hire second-best Hawkstone when the best rode beside him? Hawkstone was ready to walk away when he heard of the plan. Problem was, Black Feather intended to walk with him. According to Black Feather, the army could hire Hawkstone, and might also get Black Feather in the bargain. Or might not, if he was away. The army could not hire Black Feather without Hawkstone. Black Feather was not for hire by anyone. He rode with Hawkstone because they were blood brothers. No other reason.

And if the pair of scouts could not be enticed by gold nuggets?

The four gunmen with Isaac would have to deal out the Lord's vengeance. Hawkstone and Black Feather either worked for Isaac or they were in the way. They rode between him and that band of heathen savages now violating his precious girls. They would have to be killed.

Magruder pulled his Smith and Wesson Schofield cross-draw and checked the load. 'So, where's Iron Shirt?'

'He returns tonight,' Isaac said. 'He watches the scouts now.'

Hoback said, 'That stallion of his must be made of iron.'

Isaac Dawson looked from one to the other, then ahead where the entrance to Skeleton Canyon shimmered white in late afternoon sun. 'We will get fresh mounts when we cross into Mexico.'

Gowie turned his cross-eyes on the preacher. 'You figure we can catch them in Mexico?'

'Hopefully before,' Isaac said.

Gowie held the reins of his brown mustang as he walked. 'The only way the five of us – four of us can shoot all fifteen of them down is if we dry-gulch them. Or back shoot them, pick them off one or two at a time.'

Isaac squinted at him. 'No need to kill them all right off. We will surprise and kill as many as we can. We shoot Broken Hand then Small Dog dead. That might take the fight out of them. After we get all the weapons, we can kill the others. If it is before Mexico, it has to be quick, before the cavalry catches up. If it is in Mexico, it doesn't matter. The vengeance of the Lord is mine. You are the instruments of His wrath. We can pick them off one at a time or slaughter them all at once – however the Lord directs us.'

'Uh-huh,' Hoback said. 'What about them scouts in front of us? Between us and them heathen savages with your daughters? What you figure to do about them?'

'Buy them. They will work for me, or they will die.'

Hoback patted the neck of his appaloosa. 'Uh-huh. And who you figure will make them die if they don't want to be bought?'

'Who do you think?' Isaac said.

Hoback nodded as he looked at the ground he walked. 'Them two got a reputation. They may not be so easy to gun down. It might take all four of us. And what if they plant one or two of us in the exchange?'

Isaac stared with his thin face rock solid. 'You ask many questions, Hoback.'

'And I ain't getting no answers. I got one lightning-streak question left for you. Once we jump them heathens and start picking them off, what's to prevent the top hombre, Broken Hand, from putting a .44 or .45 slug through each pretty head of them three girls?'

Isaac Dawson stopped. 'They wouldn't dare.'

'Uh-huh. And that pretty much sums up our situation.'

In darkness, Iron Shirt rode into camp where Isaac had decided to rest for two hours, no more. Once he had the stallion tied to the string, he ignored Isaac's reproach and took two long pulls from the whiskey bottle the others shared.

'They know I'm dogging them,' he told the preacher.

Isaac closed his Bible. 'What does it matter? They are closer to the hostiles than us. If shooting breaks out, the two scouts will need our help.'

Iron Shirt squatted and helped himself to a plate of beans. 'There might not be no shooting. The two scouts split up. Black Feather rode on ahead fast, like he might mebbe parlay with Broken Hand, or Small Dog.'

Isaac frowned and leaned forward. 'And what of the other scout, the one called Hawkstone?'

Iron Shirt filled his cheeks with beans. 'I got no idea. He disappeared.'

SEVEN

Hawkstone rode east toward the Peloncillo Mountains, using the jagged foothills for protection. The chestnut picked her way among mesquite clumps and sharp rocks to double back, along the side of the canyon where Iron Shirt sometimes appeared. Early morning sun cast long shadows, making it easier for him to keep from sight. Other than the screech of birds looking for food and each other, the canyon was quiet, pronouncing the hoof scrapes of the chestnut.

Many trails angled and climbed out from the canyon floor. One or two went over the mountains into New Mexico Territory. Occasionally, Hawkstone came across the skull of a steer, from early days when Mexicans used the canyon to herd cattle north. He understood that even in the days of the early missionaries, the canyon was used as a main road into the territories from Mexico. He knew little else about the area.

Since it appeared obvious Broken Hand was headed south, he left a trail easy to follow. Yet scouts tracked him – one from the cavalry patrol, Iron Shirt for the preacher, Black Feather and Hawkstone for the army at Fort Lowell. So many scouts were not needed, not needed unless Broken Hand did not ride for Mexico. He might take any one of the trails headed east, lead his small band through the mountains into New Mexico Territory, then south to Texas. There were plenty of villages in Texas he might lose himself. He could even ride to Mexico across the Rio Grande.

But what of the girls?

Broken Hand faced three choices. Offer them for ransom, kill them, or trade them – for horses or as squaws. If for ransom, he had to contact the preacher pa, who he knew was dogging them. Maybe Black Feather might be the go-between for ransom. Or Hawkstone himself. One girl could be released to show good faith. Hawkstone felt he was missing something. There was an element about this whole business neither he nor Black Feather had figured. He did not know what it was. One thing he did know. His contract with the soldiers at Fort Lowell ended in less than two weeks. Would he break off with the kidnap band and begin pursuit of Apache Joe? His thinking leaned that way. But the pursuit of Broken Hand might be ended by then, with ransom paid – or a lot of gun smoke in the canyon. Either way, first, he would make sure Rachel and her village were safe. He needed to make a decision soon. He figured it depended on what Black Feather found.

Hawkstone found a ten-foot clearing among the rocks and stopped the chestnut. He wanted to end the noise of his own movement. He dismounted and wrapped the reins around a mesquite. The sun had moved higher with fewer shadows. The clearing showed boot-crushed cigarette butts not fragmented by rain, recent, as if somebody had watched and waited. He had a clear view of the canyon floor. Two creeks flowed slowly into an even slower river. No men or horses moved within sight. He left the chestnut tied to the mesquite while he rolled and smoked a cigarette. When he heard another horse, he slipped between sharp boulders to wait, the thong released from the hammer of his Colt.

Iron Shirt entered the clearing and yanked up his black stallion when he saw the chestnut. He pulled his Colt and peered at the rocks around him.

'I know you're here, Hawkstone. Come out so we can parlay. The preacher fella I work for wants to make a deal with you.'

Hawkstone stepped into the clearing, the Peacemaker in his hand, aimed at Iron Shirt. The stallion was huge, at least a foot taller than most horses with bulging flexing muscles and flaring nostrils, and fire in his dark eyes. In one smooth motion, Iron Shirt swung down from the saddle, his Army Colt did not waver. He was big and beefy, wearing army cast-offs and a yellow headband, his black hair to his shoulder blades streaked with gray. His eyes looked small, dark and mean. He held the reins tight as the stallion moved its large head up and down.

'What sort of deal?' Hawkstone asked.

'He'll do about anything to get them little girls back.'

Hawkstone moved beside the chestnut, the head of the horse partly between him and the Apache scout. 'That's why we're dogging the band.'

Iron Shirt took a step to the side. 'The preacher man got a pouch full of gold nuggets. He's offering nuggets to you and Black Feather, you throw in with us.'

'To do what?'

'Rescue them girls, after we slaughter all the savages.'

Hawkstone stretched tall, still partially behind the chestnut. 'Ain't you Mescalero? Ain't you one of them savages?'

'Not me, Hawkstone. I'm civilized. Even got me a white squaw.'

The black stallion pawed at the rocky ground.

'Not interested,' Hawkstone said.

'Mebbe you ought to talk it over with Black Feather. I hear he's a better scout than you anyway. He might get a different take on some real gold nuggets.'

'He won't be interested neither.'

Iron Shirt took a step forward. 'There ain't no scouting now anyway. We all know where they're headed. Once they get into Mexico they got too many directions to go. That's when we'll need tracking.'

'Unless they get jumped before Mexico.'

'That's sort of the plan.'

'Or they don't go to Mexico.'

Iron Shirt blinked with a frown. 'Why wouldn't they? Them girls is soiled now. Bucks helping themselves to the sugar. Even if Broken Hand wants to ransom them back to their pa, he knows they got a better chance in Mexico where there ain't no cavalry in the way.'

'You think the preacher will sit for any ransom demand?'

'He won't. That's why he got us. Why we got to hit

45

them before they get to Mexico.'

'There's fifteen of them, besides Small Dog and Broken Hand.'

'Young reservation Apaches, boys – up against hardened killers like us. Fifteen won't be enough for them. Our only problem is that we don't hit one of the girls. But the preacher wants your gun and Black Feather's right alongside us.'

Hawkstone noticed that Iron Hand had not cocked the hammer of his Colt yet. The stallion shook his head against the pull of the reins, which drew part of the Apache's attention.

Hawkstone reached for the reins of the chestnut and began to slowly unwrap them from the mesquite. 'You supposed to take me to the preacher so I can hear his offer?'

'Mebbe them nuggets can get you interested.'

Hawkstone stood with the reins in his hand. 'You know where he keeps the pouch too, don't you?'

Iron Shirt stepped forward. 'What do you mean by that?'

Hawkstone raised the reins to the saddle horn. When he came around to mount, he turned his back to Iron Horse. He heard the click of the Army Colt hammer. He bent and twisted with his Peacemaker aimed back, the reins in his left hand. The movement caused the stallion to jerk his head up, pulling the reins. Iron Horse shot high and to the right. Hawkstone dropped to his knees, turned and fired, the slug hitting the Apache in the belly. The shots echoed against canyon walls, the sound ricocheted from one end to the other. Iron Horse cocked again as Hawkstone's second bullet plowed through his mouth. The black stallion screamed and reared, tearing the reins out of the Apache's hands. He backed two steps and turned, already jumped at a gallop out of the clearing, weaving between boulders. Iron Shirt staggered three steps, aimed at Hawkstone to fire. Hawkstone shot him through the temple, stood, stepped toward the Apache, and shot him through the heart. His big body jerked, the Colt fell from his hand, he went down hard and fast with his head hitting a sharp rock.

White gun smoke filled the clearing. A breeze swept it away into the light blue late morning sky above the canyon. Hawkstone stood staring at the scout, waiting for his heartbeat to slow, his breathing to return to normal. He heard the clop of the stallion racing away and down the hills to the canyon floor.

Those below had no doubt heard the shots.

There were three gunmen left now.

EIGHT

Baptist preacher Isaac Dawson stood next to his gelding, which drank from a small stream near the entrance to Skeleton Canyon. The three men with him did the same. He removed his short-brimmed hat and wiped sweat from his brow with a handkerchief. It had been two days and no sign of his scout, Iron Shirt.

'What happened to him?' he asked, not expecting an intelligent answer.

Magruder stood beside his brown mustang, the mustang with its mouth in the creek. 'We heard them shots. Whatever happened ain't good.'

Isaac looked toward the canyon walls. 'We were too far away to know what direction they came from, even which side of the canyon. He might be wounded, bleeding someplace.'

Gowie adjusted his watch cap and fixed his crossed eyes on the preacher. 'In which case we ain't got to think about him no more.'

Isaac ran his gaze across the three gunfighters. 'So, if

that's what happened, who did it?'

Hoback pulled his appaloosa from the creek. 'Ain't hard to guess. He run into Hawkstone and Black Feather, one or the other, or both. Got hisself shot dead.'

Isaac frowned. 'But the black stallion of his would have run back to us.'

'Why?' Gowie said. ' 'Cause we gave such a good home to him? Lots of hay and a cool stall and surrounded by mares in season? They's plenty of places that stallion would run off to. Mebbe even that band of renegades and their pretty female ponies.'

The word 'female' triggered Isaac's thinking to his daughters. Lord, what his darling girls had to be going through. Suffering from lack of good food, no bed to sleep in, not even a change of clothes, sun heat and not enough water, and those heathen savages with their hands on them, carrying them off for carnal pleasure. They were so young, so innocent.

The fault was his. He should have been less strict, should have taught them more about the reality of living in the West, with foul-smelling men lurking in lust, and the lurid ways men looked at them with only one thing on their minds. And the Indians – he should have told them about the young bucks on the reservation with their antlers out, dreaming only of the sweet girls with their clothes off. Especially that Broken Hand, sniffing around the school like a mongrel dog, snuffling at the skirt of lovely Laura Jean, wanting to talk to her, be close enough to touch her – aching to get his hands on her. Isaac should not have just laid down rules with no explanation. He should have explained how men were when it came to blossoming girls. It was all his fault. The situation, the kidnap, the pursuit – all his fault. He had to save them, push out the horror, bring them home and back to living with the Lord. He had to redeem what was left of them for their Lord, Jesus Christ.

Most of all, he had to make certain those savages knew the blisters on their souls, over their flesh, inside their mouths. They must feel flames scorch hotter than the burning desert, eating up their hair and flesh – suffer the blazes they deserved sear their organs – they had to burn in the fires of hell, not because they were uneducated savages that knew no better, but because of what they did to his virtuous girls, and continued doing.

They could not run the horses hard anymore. Isaac had left the Bible in his saddle bag. He kept his gelding at a slow gallop as he and the three gunmen moved across the canyon floor, hearing the loping crunch of hoofs on sandy ground. The young lieutenant and his cavalry patrol were slightly more than a day behind. The land had dried. There were enough of them to show a distant dust cloud. They had picked up the pace and were closing.

The scouts, Hawkstone and Black Feather, left no trail. Maybe they were no longer on the canyon floor. Maybe they moved along the walls. For all Isaac knew, the pair might have already reached the renegade band. The band did leave traces not hard to follow, even for slow thinkers like the men with him. Too many shoeless horse prints to miss, and parts of the ground still held some moisture from recent rain. The trail continued south, as if headed directly for the Mexican border. Perhaps Lieutenant Edgar Wilson knew he was running out of time. Once the band crossed the border, he was done. Nothing more to do than turn around and ride back to Fort Huachuca or Fort Lowell, the mission a failure.

Isaac now carried less confidence in his trio of gun-fighters. He doubted the band of renegades was all young and ignorant. Older braves must have trained them in the ways of warfare. They hunted. They could ride and shoot. Some may even have experience fighting the white eyes. None would shiver in fear from three slow-thinking gunslingers, even if they had come from a reservation.

Using their scout or scouts, the band had to know what came after them. Hawkstone and Black Feather were close, or perhaps already talking with them. Isaac and his gunfighters were less than a day behind. The cavalry was less than two days back, gaining quickly. Broken Hand had to know his salvation lay in Mexico, less than a two-day hard ride ahead. Without soldiers coming after him, he would deal with gunslingers through ambush. Hide and wait, then pick them off.

Isaac Dawson slowed his fast-breathing gelding to a walk. The others slowed with him. The sun was high now, past the arc of noon, and brought enough heat to dry ground and vegetation. In less than another week, little moisture would remain. Isaac did not know how close they were to the border. No scout. Iron Shirt had either joined with Broken Hand, or run off, or got himself killed by Hawkstone and Black Feather. The shots they heard made it more likely there had been gunplay.

Once again, Isaac thought of his precious daughters, and how they were being treated. He turned to Magruder riding beside him, Magruder's head bobbing along with his mustang, half asleep, both gloved hands on the saddle horn.

'How far you think they will go?' Isaac said.

Magruder jerked his head up and looked bleary-eyed at the preacher. 'Who? What you mean?'

'Will those savages torture the girls? Will they commit unspeakable acts to them?'

Magruder looked ahead for a spell, squinting toward the expanse of canyon floor. 'Unspeakable? Depends what you mean, Parson. Unspeakable to who? I got no idea the things they do to females – besides the obvious. You got to accept them girls coming ripe, ain't no longer maidens. They've known the obvious. But I only know what Indians do to men. And some of it is unspeakable. Buried to the neck, honey on their face for red ants or scorpions. Staked with enough knife cuts to attract flesh-eating critters. Ankles tied to horses running in opposite directions. Dragged along rocky creek beds by their feet behind a horse. Gutted from navel to throat and left. Their man parts cut off and shoved down their throat. And that's besides using a knife to saw off their scalp. Them hostiles can get real creative when it comes to torture. I know they scalp women too. I seen the hair dangling on lodge poles, some of it real pretty.'

'You've lived with them?'

'Nope. But I rode with the cavalry when we wiped out every living creature in a village, even women, girls and babies. Them savages is mad for good reason. They got no place in a civilized world like we got, and some fellas think they should all be exterminated. And mebbe they will be. If not, it won't be from lack of trying.'

'How did you feel, killing women and children?'

Magruder hawked a wad of spit away to the side. He fixed his gaze on the preacher. 'I got no feelings about them. Once you start pulling the trigger and cutting them down, you only wonder about running out of ammunition, and a reload. They don't look like people no more, just wiggling, screaming targets. Mebbe you start believing what the army says, and you don't think of them as human. They's like critters running the plains, like buffalo and antelope and goats and pigs. Nobody is gonna punish you for shooting them. And that sets in your mind. They's fair game. You ain't gonna be arrested and sent to jail. It changes the way men think. They's too many of them and they's a problem – the Indian problem – and we got to kill off as many as we can to help solve the problem. No matter how many you shoot, nobody cares. You got a clear conscience 'cause nobody points a finger at you, and you can shoot as many as you got cartridges for. If you see a heathen maiden you take a fancy to, you can help yourself to that too, then shoot her.'

Isaac felt a veil of doom for his lovely girls. 'My Lord,' was all he could say.

'Yup,' Magruder said, 'like I told you, Parson, them heathens got good reason to be mad.'

NINE

Beside another nameless stream flowing toward a river –
soon to be dried up – Hawkstone knelt next to the
morning campfire waiting for Arbuckle coffee to boil.
He also waited for his blood brother, Black Feather.
Black Feather had talked with Broken Hand. There was
to be a meeting, not with Broken Hand, but with Laura
Jean Dawson.

Hawkstone knew he was surrounded by the band. He
felt their presence around him. They made no move
toward him, but the rawhide loop was off the hammer of
his Colt. He felt no anxiety or fear because Black Feather
said it would be all right. He felt anticipation, and curios-
ity. Men already had their minds fixed on what was
happening among the renegade band of Apaches – especially to the girls. He was there to find the truth of it,
among other trails. He squatted less than a day from the
Mexican border. The preacher pa was a day behind,
coming fast. Black Feather said the lieutenant and his
ten soldiers were closing faster, another half day behind.

And Apache Joe was out there in the territories,

spreading disease and death.

Hawkstone hardly expected to be alone with Laura Jean. She came from the rocks and entered his campsite, also appearing expectant. She looked like an Indian princess, except for her ragged store-bought dress and the wispy strands of her long raven hair. Her lovely face was flushed from hard daytime riding. And she was not alone. Stepping next to her was a young warrior, just under six feet, slim, shirtless, thick black hair with a band that held three eagle feathers. His hand was on her elbow. They walked together. On the other side of her, Black Feather moved in equal liquid motion with the warrior.

Hawkstone nodded to the warrior. 'You are Broken Hand.' It was not a question.

Broken Hand returned the nod, his face somber, without telling expression. It was then the twisted left hand could be seen – not as a claw, but slightly bent, mis-shapen. He kept it at his side, not hiding it.

The sisters followed and kept toward the outside of the camp. One looked nervous and chubby, stared at her tattered shoes. Her hair was in a tight bun. She glanced up at Hawkstone, who stood by the campfire.

'I am Edna,' she said. 'Praise Jesus. We are saved.'

Hawkstone turned to the other sister, tiny, sprightly, long blonde hair, with a smile that could be taken as a smirk, a teaser. She, too, looked trail worn. Her petulant face moved from one man to another, her gaze passed over her sisters.

Hawkstone said, 'That makes you Lucille.'

'We're not going back to him,' Lucille said. Her little

mouth tightened with determination.

'Yes, we are,' Edna said. 'We're going home.'

Hawkstone squinted at her, then at Lucille. 'Ain't your say, ladies.'

Laura Jean took a step toward Hawkstone. 'It is certainly *my* say. *I'll* determine where I go.'

Broken Hand stepped beside her. She wrapped herself around his arm. He couldn't have been more than twenty. His young dark eyes stared at Hawkstone. 'She comes with me.'

Laura Jean hugged closer. 'I'm his woman. I go where he goes.'

Black Feather squatted to pull the coffee pot from the fire. He looked up at Hawkstone. 'You see how it is.'

'I am Small Dog,' a brave said as he joined them. He did look small, shorter than Laura Jean, shirtless, with hard muscles and a scowl. After looking around at the others, he focused on Hawkstone. 'Why do we talk with you?'

Hawkstone ignored him and turned to Broken Hand. 'Will you wait for their pa?'

'No.'

Black Feather set the coffee pot on the ground and rose to stand beside Hawkstone. He concentrated on Broken Hand. 'We spoke of this.'

'We spoke of the younger sisters. Laura Jean comes to Mexico with me.'

Laura Jean put her arms around his waist, her face against his chest, while looking at Hawkstone. 'I love him.'

Edna said, 'Don't talk like that. Daddy is coming and

we're going home.'

'I *am* home. I've had enough switches on my bare bottom and the Bible shoved down my throat. No more.'

Edna stepped with marching steps to her sister. 'You've strayed from Jesus Christ, our Savior. You must come home, Laura Jean, come back to the Lord – redeem yourself for your fornication with this savage.'

Laura Jean kept hugging Broken Hand as she glared at her sister. 'I love you, Edna, but your head is as twisted as Pa's.'

'I'm coming with you, Laura Jean,' the tiny sister, Lucille said.

'No, you're not.'

'I want my own warrior,' Lucille said.

Hawkstone turned his back to them and looked at Black Feather straight. 'What the hell is this?'

'Not what their pa expected.'

Broken Hand untangled himself from Laura Jean's arms and motioned to Small Dog. 'Come, my brother, we will talk to these men.'

'No,' Laura Jean said with a pout. 'Don't leave me.'

'Wait by the horses. Take your sisters with you. We will decide what is to be done.'

They walked upstream along the creek, Small Dog and Broken Hand in the lead, Hawkstone and Black Feather following.

Broken Hand turned back, his young dark eyes on Hawkstone. 'The sisters were not supposed to be here. Laura Jean and I planned to leave, but they were with her and we took them along.'

'Then you will release the sisters, Edna and Lucille?'

57

'Yes. Once we are in Mexico, my men will join Geronimo at Canyon de los Embudos. Laura Jean and me go to the coast of the inland sea, to an Apache village just south of Caborca Puerto Peñasco. The Mexicans will not bother us. We will live a happy life fishing and hunting.'

Hawkstone studied the sharp honest young face. 'You do not ask ransom for the girls? The preacher pa has gold.'

'I do not want his gold. I only take Laura Jean.'

Hawkstone said, 'Her pa will want all three girls.'

'She is my woman. She belongs with me. I want no more white man and fighting. I want no more reservation. Now I will live by the work of my hands. I will provide for my woman and me without government handouts.'

Black Feather stood by the creek, looking across, and said nothing.

Small Dog looked up from Broken Hand to Hawkstone. 'I go back to my village. Apache Joe is close. My woman is there heavy with child. I should not have gone away from her. I am stupid and she weeps for me in our tepee.'

Black Feather turned away from the creek. 'Where is your village?'

'It is one day from Fort Sumner.'

Hawkstone said, 'In New Mexico Territory. Last I heard, Apache Joe is west of there, headed toward Fort McLane.'

Small Dog said. 'The boy, Patch Green Leaf rode to us from Fort Huachuca and told us of Apache Joe. He has passed Fort McLane. He has left disease and death behind him.'

Hawkstone stared. 'How did the boy get past the cavalry and the gunmen and us?'

'It was not hard.'

A brave joined the group, his dark eyes on Hawkstone. Broken Hand held his palm up. 'What is it, Running Wolf?'

The brave was as tall as Broken Hand but skinny, and older, maybe close to thirty. 'I will talk to the one called Hawkstone.'

'What is it?' Hawkstone asked.

Instead, Broken Hand said, 'In New Mexico Territory, Running Wolf knew the squaw, the woman who rides with Apache Joe.'

Running Wolf stepped closer to Hawkstone. 'Before the disease, before the tattoos and Apache Joe, she was a girl with smiles, and giving. She was Looking Glass, a Choctaw princess.'

Hawkstone squinted at the brave. 'How well did you know her?'

'We were easy friends, nothing more. I have woman now. I have two sons.'

Hawkstone turned to the others then back to Running Wolf. 'Then why tell me this?'

'So, you know. So, you learn Tattoo was not always as she is now, full of hate.'

As Running Wolf walked away, Black Feather stepped to Hawkstone and put a hand on the arm of his blood brother. 'We should not be here. We should be riding for Little Rain and Rachel. Apache Joe may have already passed by.'

'He has,' Small Dog said. 'The wire talk at Fort Huachuca says typhoid fever is at Fort Sumner. The cavalry sent to arrest Apache Joe have disease. There are ten with smallpox at Fort McLane. I leave tomorrow – over the mountains for my village. I must hurry to my woman.'

Hawkstone stood silent. His contract with the army ended in three days. Black Feather was right. They should be riding north hard. The moral duty and self-imposed rules of the cavalry pushed the army above killing on sight, except for certain Indian villages. And they would die of disease for it. For all he knew, Apache Joe may have visited the village before he warned them. Rachel would stay. She would help those infected until she was too tired to stand. Yes, Black Feather was right, as always. Their business here was done. Any contract he had ended now.

He turned to Broken Hand. 'Put Lucille and Edna on horses. Black Feather and me will ride them north to their pa. You ride hard for the border, get you and your woman to the village by the inland sea.'

Broken Hand put his twisted hand on Hawkstone's shoulder. 'What of the gunmen riding with the preacher?'

Hawkstone sighed. 'Me and Black Feather will take care of them.'

TEN

Laura Jean had hugged her sisters and wished them happiness. She appeared content but carried the expression of a girl with much to do. Her lovely faced filled with love when she looked at Broken Hand. As for Broken Hand, he bid farewell to Small Dog and watched the brave ride out of camp at a gallop. He gave Hawkstone and Black Feather a nod as he helped Laura Jean to mount her pony then threw his leg over his own pinto. They rode south at first light, with Running Wolf and the band of braves following.

An hour later, the others broke camp and rode north. They rode single-file, Black Feather in the lead, Hawkstone bringing up the rear, the girls between them. The girls churned in their own thoughts, Edna looking ahead with anticipation, Lucille sullen. Hawkstone was not sure what kind of greeting they would get from the preacher, since they would arrive one daughter short. He only knew he did not intend to linger. Other priorities clawed at him.

The morning sun was not high enough, so they rode within the shadows of the Peloncillo Mountains, which brought a chill to the air. The landscape spread shiny with dew. Two hawks circled high, looking for the skitter of small animals. For the first hour, they only heard the clomp of walking horses.

'I have to pee,' Lucille said. 'When do we breakfast?'

Edna said, 'Lucille, be quiet. We're going home to our daddy.'

Lucille scowled at her sister. 'I still have to pee.'

Hawkstone eased up the chestnut. Ahead, Black Feather stopped.

'There's a clump of mesquite out there on the left. Both of you go.'

'I don't have to,' Edna said.

Hawkstone sighed. 'Of course you don't. But you will soon as we're moving again. Make an effort.'

The girls slid down from their ponies in their soiled, torn dresses, and high-stepped around the back of the mesquite.

Black Feather relaxed on his pinto. 'We could just wait for the pa to catch up. I figure two or three hours.'

'We keep going, we can cut that in half.'

Black Feather nodded. 'We go to your village first. Beyond that we pick up the trail of Apache Joe.'

Hawkstone looked to the south. 'He might run back to Mexico. He knows the cavalry is after him.'

'First, you and me better think of the men with the preacher pa.'

'I ain't forgot them.'

Black Feather looked off toward the mesquite bush. 'I

do not think the preacher will accept just the two girls.'

'Me neither.'

'You got a Ben Franklyn to tell us why?'

Hawkstone thought as he rubbed his hand across his mouth. '*The way to see by faith is to shut the eye of reason.*' Hawkstone knew they announced their coming to Isaac Dawson, the preacher pa of the two girls. He figured the gunmen would scatter and hide, ready to start shooting, but the three likely would not open fire with the girls riding along. The sun was at high noon when they rode into the camp.

'I'm hungry,' Lucille said.

'Shut up,' Edna told her.

The preacher and his three men had only stopped for coffee and beans – a noon meal – to get something in their bellies for a lot more riding ahead. The fire was out and they were ready to mount and ride on. Spaced in a circle of about twenty feet, they turned from their mounts in surprise. The preacher had a thin face and a big nose with his dark eyes close together. His brow creased and his eyebrows raised. He smiled with joy at seeing the girls. The other three bent slightly, left hand holding reins, right hand on the grips of their weapons.

Edna was the first off her horse. She jumped down and ran to her pa. 'Pa,' she cried. 'Pa.' She threw her arms around his neck and almost knocked him over.

'Edna. . . .' he said, blinking. He looked up. 'Lucille?' He looked beyond Lucille. 'Where is Laura Jean?' It was then he turned to Hawkstone. 'Oh, no. She isn't . . they didn't . . . Oh, God.'

'She rode to Mexico with Broken Hand,' Hawkstone said.

'What?' the preacher cried, frowning under his flat-topped short-brimmed hat. 'What did you say?'

Hawkstone watched the three gunmen who had not moved. 'She's in love. By now they're close to the border.' Hawkstone and Black Feather still sat their mounts. Nobody had invited them to step down. Like Hawkstone, Black Feather kept his gaze on the three gunmen, going from one to the other and back again.

Lucille slowly dismounted and walked to her pa who embraced her next to Edna.

The preacher looked up at Hawkstone. 'I am Isaac Dawson. These men work for me.'

'Tell them to get their hands off them hog legs.'

'Or else what?' a cross-eyed jasper in a woollen cap said. His hand did not move.

Hawkstone removed the rawhide thong. 'Or else them girls might get hit by stray bullets.'

Isaac Dawson waved a hand. 'Enough. I want no gunplay here. You boys ease off.' To Hawkstone, he said, 'We still got a way to go. Laura Jean is not living in Mexico with some savage. Do you know where they're headed?'

Hawkstone kept his gaze on the cross-eyed man, who, of the three, still had his hand on his weapon. 'Dawson, take your two girls and go home. Be grateful what you got.'

'Never, sir. I intend to retrieve *all* my kidnapped girls.'

'Laura Jean wasn't kidnapped. She come of her own accord. Let them be.'

'Nonsense. She is still being held captive.'

'She ain't,' Hawkstone said. He heard a noise, the metallic rattle of fast riding soldiers. The noise was faint, coming from the north.

But, as what sometimes happened in such situations, something innocent set off a series of events that could not be prevented nor reversed. In the brief seconds of quiet tension, a prairie dog ran across the center of the campsite and between the legs of Isaac Dawson's gelding. The horse bucked and threw its head around. The cross-eyed jasper drew his Army Colt and fired at Hawkstone. Hawkstone heard the whizz of the bullet and felt a chip tear out of his vest under his left arm. By then he had his Colt cocked and aimed and shot the jasper in the forehead just above the bridge of his nose under his woolen cap. The cross-eyed gunman's eyes opened wide in surprise as he jerked back and down. He lifted his weapon to fire again but it fell to the ground beside him, and he laid flat.

'Stop!' Isaac Dawson cried.

The other two had quickly grabbed at their weapons. Black Feather dropped one who was drawing a Smith and Wesson Schofield with a shot to the chest. The third gunmen drew too fast and his Colt fired before he could aim. The shot caused Edna to yelp, spin and claw at her pa as she slid down against him. That encouraged Dawson to pull his weapon, but Hawkstone had already shot the gunman in the chest and belly. Horses stomped and jumped. As the gunman stumbled back against his appaloosa he fired again, wild and low, and hit the preacher high in the left leg. Lucille screamed, then again, over and over. Air pounding with gunshots suddenly turned quiet, except for female screams, and noises of the cavalry riding into the camp. Three gunmen were down, their horses still running away, just slowing from a gallop in fear. Two cavalry soldiers chased down the two ponies of the girls and returned them.

The preacher sat beside his gelding, head down, left hand still holding reins, right hand around the back of Edna, holding her tight against him. Lucille stood next to the cold camp ashes, hands against her ears, screaming again and again. Ten soldiers rode into camp, spread to surround it, rifles aimed at Hawkstone and Black Feather.

ELEVEN

It took most of the afternoon for Hawkstone and Black Feather to unravel themselves from Lieutenant Edgar Wilson and his army regulations.

'You got two more days left on your contract,' the lieutenant said to Hawkstone. 'You know where Broken Hand went.'

'The contract is done,' Hawkstone said.

The preacher had his leg wrapped. Edna had been shot in the shoulder, a flesh wound, not enough to keep her from riding. Her chubby face still showed relief to be next to her pa. Cavalry burial detail was taking care of the three dead gunmen. Lucille calmed enough to sit on a rock weeping, her hands clutched together in her lap, her body shaking from likely thinking on what happened and what might have happened.

Lieutenant Edgar Wilson and his troops looked trail weary from days of hard riding. He rode a tired white mustang of mixed breed. He was just over twenty, school-boy faced with ordinary brown hair – everything about him looked young, inexperienced, and ordinary. His troops moved as slow as their worn-out horses. All they seemed to care about was a place to sit, a drink from their canteen, a smoke, and to close their eyes. They were young, many likely recruits from forts east, or forts still standing after the war, brought west to kill Indians. They lounged around the edges of the campsite. Three had already spread out to sleep.

Hawkstone and Black Feather were ready to mount and ride on out.

'You still belong to the army,' the lieutenant said to Hawkstone, 'still technically a scout for the cavalry. For two days more you are under my command. You signed a contract, mister, and it is binding.' He tried to bring authority into his young voice but it didn't reach.

'Write me up if you want to, boy. This campaign is done. The band with Broken Hand is on their way to join Geronimo. Broken Hand is in Mexico with Laura Jean – and that's the end of it. I'm going after Apache Joe.'

Hawkstone saw the fight had gone out of the preacher. His thin face had every feature turned down, his mouth fixed in a scowl. His gunmen were dead. His leg had to be giving him some bother. He had to live with Edna getting herself shot, and Lucille seeing gun killing that sent her into hysterics.

Hawkstone mounted along with Black Feather.

The young lieutenant squinted against the sun, making his face look younger. 'You're riding into court martial, Hawkstone. I can hold you here under arrest.'

Hawkstone hadn't reloaded and he wanted no battle with the army. He placed his hand on the Colt, the rawhide loop still off.

'Don't try, soldier boy. You got the responsibility of a wounded girl, an hysterical girl, their shot pa, and worn-out troops. Get them all to Fort Huachuca so they can rest and move on from this – so you can move on. The thing is done. There ain't no more chase.'

Isaac Dawson limped one step from his horse and stared at Hawkstone. 'It is not done, sir. I will keep trying to rescue Laura Jean.'

Hawkstone returned the stare. 'Good luck with that kind of thinking, Parson. You best look after the girls you have. Sorry about your oldest.' He heeled the chestnut and touched the brim of his hat to the girls.

He and Black Feather rode out of camp with no more talk.

They rode a light gallop through Apache Pass directly for what was left of Fort Thomas. While Hawkstone reckoned the lieutenant and his charges might head straight for Fort Huachuca, he and Black Feather bypassed the fort, and approached Fort Lowell. Maybe disease had not hit everybody at the fort yet, but typhoid and smallpox had swept through the outside tepees like a dry sage fire. Many Indians had left, likely spreading disease farther. Those who died had been buried in mass graves with limestone shoveled over them. No tepees were left standing, the ground charred black with a few dark sticks standing.

Wearing bandanas over their faces, Hawkstone and Black Feather kept back from charred earth. Hawkstone wanted information but intended to go no closer. There was nobody within sight. The fort stood gray in an afternoon with clouds above blocking any brightness.

Chimney smoke could be seen from inside the fort. The smell of living people drifted out to them – cooking meat, outhouse aromas, animals – dogs, pigs, goats, and horses – man sweat, and sweet woman perfume. As they sat their ponies, the gate opened and a rider came out, heeling his mount hard. He galloped straight for them looking determined but with no weapon. Hawkstone released the loop on his Colt.

'You can't come into the fort,' the man shouted. Then, as he drew close to them, he reined in. 'You stay away. Can't come in.'

Hawkstone said, 'Ain't got no intention going in. How bad is it?'

He was a boy, not a man – his felt hat was wide-brimmed and badly shaped. Maybe not much over fifteen, a red and green kerchief covered his chin, pulled down from his nose and mouth. The rest of his shiny face needed soap and water. He looked from one to the other with squinty brown eyes that showed little sleep.

'They talking of burning down the fort. I ain't caught nothing but it took my ma and pa and my two little brothers.'

'Was Apache Joe here?' Hawkstone asked.

The boy blinked. 'Don't know. I heard of him, the blanket trader, Apache Joe.' He turned his head to look at the charred land. 'Mebbe he visited them Apache outside, mebbe brought disease and give it to them, and they come in the fort and spread it.'

Hawkstone's look followed the boy's gaze. 'Or men from the fort came outside for visits.'

The boy frowned. 'Visits. What for, visits?'

'Some of them Apache girls look mighty inviting.'

'Boy, ain't that the truth.' He sat straight in the saddle. 'You mean for hugging and kissing and such?'

'And such,' Black Feather said.

The boy looked from one to the other. 'You think that's how disease got in the fort? I mean, we already had malaria, but not big, not like the other that spread to almost everybody. I think the doc said the malaria was under control. But typhoid and smallpox, and who knows what else, just hit and spread quick. Seemed like everybody had it, and they was dying every place you turned.'

Hawkstone said, 'Who burned the little village? Soldiers?'

'Yes, sir. They buried the bodies and torched the tepees. Got three cavalry patrols out there doing the same. I hear tell other forts sent out patrols too. It's like they going to burn every Apache village touched by them diseases.'

Hawkstone and Black Feather exchanged glances. Hawkstone felt pressure push inside his chest.

'We'll be moving along, boy,' Hawkstone said.

The boy's face wrinkled as if he was about to cry. 'Take me with you.'

'No.'

The boy moved his mount closer. 'I'm strong and I shoot good. I used to buffalo hunt with my pa. I'm a good worker. I can pack a mule and fetch firewood and do any work you fellas want me to. I got nobody now. You wouldn't be sorry.'

Black Feather had already turned his pony away.

Hawkstone looked sternly into the tired young brown eyes. 'We're on a killing hunt, boy. We intend to hunt Apache Joe to ground and shoot him down like a buffalo. No conversation. We ain't got room for no boy.'

'Please, sir.'

By then Hawkstone and Black Feather were riding north at a gallop.

TWELVE

It was a three day ride to reach the banks of the San Pedro River northeast of Tucson. Rain began light but poured heavy the second day away from the boy. Hawkstone and Black Feather camped on the bank of the river under a heavy growth of willows with canvas over them.

The fourth day, rain clouds drifted away and brought late spring heat. They found another burned down village.

With their faces covered, they rode around the ashes. They searched the ground seeking any sign of Apache Joe. The pressure in Hawkstone's chest grew. It climbed to his throat and threatened to close it and made him swallow often. He kept blinking hard. He studied the ghost of the village and conjured thoughts about his own he did not want to imagine. They were still a day's ride to Fort McLane, then a day more to the Chiricahua village and Rachel.

They separated and rode wide around the ashes, staring at the ground, still within sight of each other so they did not have to shout. Hawkstone saw so many prints from cavalry horses he could not clearly pick out shoeless Apache ponies. Rain and army horses had apparently wiped out any sign of Apache Joe.

Black Feather said, 'We must widen the circle. The army followed trails. We must look beyond what is busy.'

Prints moved away from the village toward Fort McLane. Hawkstone walked his chestnut to the west, away from the fort trail, among thick growths of mesquite and juniper trees. He saw no tracks outside the main trails. 'He could have been here months ago.'

'Yes. But he would leave something, a sign. The fire was less than two days after the rain. Army tracks are fresh. You must think, my brother. Apache Joe might have traded with your village before you were there. He might have traded with warriors from your village who took the disease back. Your warning came too late. The disease was already there.'

Hawkstone found it hard to swallow. His breathing quickened. 'Are you telling me we're too late?'

'We cannot know until we are there. The medicine woman may have left the village.'

Hawkstone shook his head. 'No, she would stay. She would keep helping until it was too late for her.'

'And Little Rain?'

'She would stand by Rachel's side.'

Black Feather swung down off his pinto. 'I have found something.'

Hawkstone walked the chestnut to the pinto and dismounted. He squatted beside Black Feather, studied the ground. He said, 'I figure some of the hides and blankets got from this village to Fort McLane. Mebbe Apache Joe never went to the fort. All he'd need is for his blankets to get there.'

Black Feather pointed to the damp ground. 'See the small puddles. These are ponies without metal shoes, before the rain.'

'Looks like a small band.'

'No. Four horses. Apache Joe rides one. Tattoo another. They pull two pack horses with blankets and hides. Four horses.'

Hawkstone stood and stared at the fuzzy prints worn by time and rain, that barely indented the ground. He looked up in the direction they were headed. 'How long ago?'

Black Feather shrugged. 'A month, maybe two.'

Hawkstone stood. 'They're headed northwest.'

Black Feather stood and nodded. 'Old prints. They do not go to Fort McLane. They lead toward the village of the medicine woman.'

Anson Hawkstone and Black Feather saw smoke curl from the horizon in front of them. As they heeled their mounts, flames became visible. The fire engulfed the entire village, bringing the stench of burning flesh, and the smell of scorched hides used for tepees and clothes.

Soldiers off their horses, faces covered with bandanas circled the flames with shovels to keep the fire from spreading to the prairie. A mound of piled earth the size of a Conestoga wagon rose just north of the fire. Men still shoveled dirt onto it.

Hawkstone rode a wide circle to the end of the village where Rachel's hut had once stood. There was no hut. Flames cracked as they ate every structure around it, even the chairs that had sat against the wall, even the chair Hawkstone had built to sit beside her. By this time, nothing in the inferno rose higher than his stirrups.

A soldier came by with a shovel. He also carried a bucket half filled with water to use against escaping embers. His eyes were two small pools of blood from smoke and fatigue. 'Better push back, sir. If it spreads, I ain't got enough shovel or water to quench it.'

'What of the medicine woman? Her hut was over there.'

The soldier nodded to the mound of earth. 'She was the last to catch it. She went with the others.'

Hawkstone felt his forehead tingle, his face burned flush, only partly from the flames. The pressure in his chest crushed his heart until he felt a deep ache inside. 'Are you sure?'

'Ask the doc. He's out by the tent.'

Black Feather waited as Hawkstone rode back. He was silent. Hawkstone's face answered any questions.

'There's a tent,' Hawkstone said.

Black Feather pointed to the northwest from the fire. Two lines of army tents began fifty yards out from the flames. One tent was bigger than the other white A-shaped shelters. They rode around the fire to the largest tent, and dismounted. Soldiers on foot moved back and forth to the fire with their shovels. The few buckets were filled from a barrel that made trips to the river.

A major sat in front of the big tent with a large cigar and a glass of amber liquid. His fleshy face carried soot and the flush of heat.

In a chair next to him sat a heavily-mustached man in a white coat turned gray with smoke, also with a whiskey glass. He looked small as a woman with delicate hands. He was saying, 'Yup, back during medieval times – the plague, caused by rats. Before it was done it wiped out one-third of humanity in England. Could be we got us a plague here, Major.'

'I'm asking after the medicine woman,' Hawkstone said.

The major took a sip and cocked his military cap to his left. 'Ask the doc, there. He was with them to the end. Them still sick and alive we got gathered in a camp a mile from here.'

'Rachel is not with them,' the doctor said. He squinted at Hawkstone. 'You a friend?'

'Yes.'

He shook his head. His thin bird face also was coated with soot. 'Don't know why I never got it. She was by my side during the worst of it.' He turned to look at the flames. 'We tried to get all the dead buried, tried to get them out. Some are still in there. You can smell them. Rachel caught the typhoid – bloody nose, the fever, the headache, muscle pain, bloating, vomiting, the rose-colored blisters on her body. We had to put her with the others.' He nodded to the earth mound. 'I wanted to dig a grave just for her, she gave so much helping those poor souls. Just not enough time, and so many – small-pox, typhoid. And it's still spreading, especially the smallpox.'

Hawkstone leaned toward the man. 'Are you sure it

was Rachel?'

The doctor leaned back away from him. 'No man could forget that flaming red hair. She was a fine-looking woman.'

Black Feather said, 'There was a girl with her, a young Apache, Little Rain.'

But the doctor stared at the mound. 'Infected drinking water. And the blankets. Somebody gets the disease and uses a tree or open prairie to do his squat. Flies and other insects land on the leavings then buzz to food or water, or lights on another not infected, and does its business. We whites got outhouses. It's still unsanitary, but not open like these people.' He stared at his sooty shoes. 'We're such a filthy race of people. We don't bathe enough, or wear clean clothes, or boil water to drink. We contaminate everything we touch. We live worse than animals.'

'What about the girl?' Hawkstone asked.

The doctor shook his head. 'Didn't see no girl.' He frowned. 'Come to think on it, at the beginning there was an old man, shriveled on a swayback pinto.'

'Moving Rock,' Hawkstone said.

The doctor took a sip from his glass. 'I think he took her off with him, the young girl, maybe he was her grandpa.'

'Took her where?' Black Feather asked.

The doctor shrugged. 'I had enough to keep me busy. Nothing I could do to stop it, or cure it. Just tried to keep clean water over them and in them. It was nothing. The medicine woman stood next to me helping. None of us could do nothing, except watch them suffer and die.' He raised his bloodshot eyes to Hawkstone. 'Yes, Rachel was one of them. She suffered and she died. And she is buried out there with all them others.'

THIRTEEN

Hawkstone had thought of the worst that could happen, and the worst had happened. He and Black Feather rode among those still barely alive, carrying false hope, then away from the flames, back to the San Pedro river and along its banks. The chestnut walked and he sat in the saddle following the pinto.

Feelings inside him began to slip away, down to his guts and out and gone. Gone was the flutter of anticipation, the not knowing. He knew without doubt. There was no question now. His Rachel was gone forever. No more touching her, holding her, soft talk with her – just looking at her. No sea-going life with her sharing his captain's cabin, voyaging the world carrying trade goods. Love, hate, revenge – emotions he might have once felt swept out of him. In their wake, feelings and emotions left his insides hollow. In his chest was the same emptiness he carried when his wife and boy were blown up during that bank robbery so many years ago. His thoughts were the same as then, when he found the robbers and killed them without mercy, even the boy riding with them – when he became no good and turned outlaw, killing and robbing without cause or reason. Thinking of any future clogged his throat.

Without Rachel, he had no future, none at all. Even his hatred for Apache Joe emptied. Would killing him and his squaw bring Rachel back? What was the point? To stop the renegade from infecting others? What did it matter? The others were strangers to him. The object of his love had died. He cared nothing for others around him. Others could take care of Apache Joe. It was not up to him. He didn't care.

Hours passed without him thinking on time. The day wore down and faded to gray then dark. Hawkstone looked at the river beside them as he walked the chestnut and thought nothing. It was just water flowing from one place to another. He sighed. Ah, what did anything matter? His gaze fell to the back of Black Feather. His blood brother seemed to be studying the bank as they rode. The night became too dark to see him clearly. He was still tracking, still seeking answers or direction or following somebody. What for? There was no more reason for living, no life left. The village was gone, the hut burned level to the ground. Rachel Cleary, Rachel Good Squaw, the medicine woman, the woman of Anson Hawkstone had died horribly.

'Just ahead,' Black Feather said. 'They have camp just around the bend. Can you smell the cooking rabbit, Hawkstone?'

'Ah, it doesn't matter, nothing does.'

Black Feather fixed him with a stare he barely saw in the darkness. 'Everything matters, Hawkstone. Life begins and life ends. It is the way of living. We all matter, but only to a few, and only for a short time.'

'Who are you tracking?'

'We are here.'

They rode into the camp of Moving Rock and Little Rain. The old warrior growled at the invasion. The girl, Little Rain, looked at Hawkstone and Black Feather, and her lovely face beamed with a smile in campfire light. The smile reminded Hawkstone of Rachel.

When they had each eaten a little of the rabbit, Hawkstone found his bottle of whiskey and moved, brooding, away from the others. Moving Rock sat with knees bent, ankles crossed, minding the fire. Little Rain sat close to Black Feather. Hawkstone felt they looked good together. They belonged together.

Moving Rock's creased face squinted across the fire at Hawkstone. 'I told you.'

'Quiet, old man,' Hawkstone said.

'I told you not to chase after pretty girls. Apache Joe is active and he leaves death behind him.'

Hawkstone sipped his whiskey. He offered none to anyone else. 'You don't get it, old man. Rachel is dead. Soldiers buried her with the other dead. Her body lies in a ditch with diseased Apache.'

They sat silent. Hawkstone was not yet at a point where he could think of anything other than his own selfish personal grief, his loss, what he would miss about her, how her death emptied any future plans. He feared his past would return, that the emptiness inside him would be replaced by a burning hatred, not aimed at just

Apache Joe, but aimed at everything and everybody around him.

The same kind of hatred he had felt when he was sent to prison.

Inside prison walls, in his 5 x 5 x 7 room – (no talking – one chamber pot, one nightstand, one cot – ordered to air bedding twice a week – bathe and change; underwear once a week) – he had met men just like him, men complaining about the bad life others had caused, men who grumbled about how others had put them where they were, and made them what they were – men who hated one individual, usually a man in authority, a father, an older brother, a banker – or a woman. Always, it was the others who had ruined their lives and put them where they were now, locked behind bars.

Hawkstone had been no different.

And now, as he sat in campfire light, drinking his whiskey, he blamed spirits, gods, chance, luck – he knew his thinking was tainted by tragedy. He was that other killing animal out there, against everything and everyone. Somehow, they had taken his Rachel from him, and he didn't give a tobacco spit at a spittoon for any of them. He hated them all. And at the top of the list was indeed, Apache Joe.

'How do we get him?' he said.

The other three remained silent.

By her fawning, touching, wiggling gestures, it was obvious Little Rain wanted to be alone with Black Feather. Black Feather eased her aside enough to study Hawkstone.

Moving Rock turned his creaky gaze to Hawkstone.

'There are vigilantes. They hunt Apache Joe and his squaw, Tattoo.'

Hawkstone frowned at Black Feather. 'Did you know of vigilantes?'

'Only by rumor. They are not good men.'

Hawkstone drained the last of his whiskey. 'Even better. Let them slaughter the renegade and catch disease and they all die covered in blood red blisters. But only after they murder Apache Joe and burn and bury his body. His squaw too.'

Moving Rock poked the campfire with a limb. 'Does Hawkstone find the vigilantes?'

Hawkstone felt himself nodding from the effects of demon whiskey. 'Hawkstone finds nobody. Hawkstone searches nowhere. Hawkstone rides alone.'

'To where?' Black Feather said.

'To nowhere.'

'I ride with you. We ride together, like always.'

Hawkstone shook his head. 'Not like always. There will never be like always again. You stay with Little Rain. That is your place. I stay with demons and devils. That is my place.'

Little Rain raised to her knees and faced Hawkstone, her child-woman face streaked with tears. 'We all miss her. We all feel the absence. This did not just happen to you.'

'Me most,' Hawkstone said.

'Because you take it inside you badly,' Little Rain said.

'Yes'm, I take it badly. I now know being a good man was temporary for me. I am the man who robbed banks and killed and went to prison. That is the man I am. I tried to be the other. Rachel made me want to be honorable, but it was temporary because that ain't who I am. I ain't honorable, I'm as evil in my way as Apache Joe is in his.'

Old Moving Rock said, 'The whiskey talks louder than your brain, Hawkstone.'

Hawkstone pushed himself to stand. 'I'm riding the lonesome trail for a spell. I got a Ben Franklyn for you. *There are no ugly loves, nor handsome prisons.* You can all think on that.' He staggered to the chestnut and with some trouble, mounted. He rode away without a backward look.

FOURTEEN

Anson Hawkstone stretched upon a cot, his head on a filthy pillow. He lay on his left side, holding the opium pipe loose. On another cot opposite him lay a wrinkled bald Chinese man who also held a pipe. An oiled-filled lantern hung between them, putting out a pathetic pale-yellow glow. Between them on the floor, they each had their open quart jar with small smoking thimbles of dark semi-fluid inside. The room, about fifteen-feet square with a dozen cots in two rows, connected behind a Chinese laundry. Only three cots were empty. The room was smoky and hot, carrying the smell of opium smoke and unwashed men, making Hawkstone sweat. Men coughed, some groaned. The laundry room in front sat along narrow China Town Alley off Washington Street near downtown Tucson. Clapboard buildings on each side stood three storeys high. Windows were open which allowed Chinese language voices to carry along the alley. Summer was all but gone.

That was what Hawkstone remembered. He had not had another clear thought in weeks.

Through a murky haze, he relived worthless years that

had been his life over and over. He did it for self-pity, so he could continue to feel sorry for himself. Since he was worthless, it was fitting he should lose any small grasp he might have had at a satisfying life. He had not gone on a rampage of killing because in those early days he had been very young and very stupid. He was older now and he chose to wallow in himself and churn over how badly life had treated him. That kind of thinking required little effort. He did not have to draw his Colt and shoot anybody. He could lie on the cot and inhale opium and never have to leave the inside of his head.

Mia Chang, the Opium Girl, looked after him. She was more than the Opium Girl. She had told him that in her small village near Hong Kong, her father suffered a devastating fire that destroyed his restaurant. Without money or business, he was forced to sell his two youngest daughters. When they arrived in Arizona Territory, the sisters were separated and never saw each other again. Mia Chang came to the laundry in Tucson for work but was quickly made a sing-song girl and moved with other girls to the house of Kin Duc. Now, as an added duty, she came to the opium den behind the laundry, operated by the seventh mistress of Kin Duc. Not yet twenty, she allowed Hawkstone to slide his hand along her bare leg under her clothing. She hugged him when he told her he needed it. Her intimate sweetness – which he declined – carried a price of two dollars, and on occasion, she admonished him.

'Look at you, Hawkstone. How can I give myself to you completely when you are like this? You do not belong here. This is where old men come to waste the end of their lives.' She nodded to the aged Chinese man across from him. 'His stomach is eaten up, passages closed by growth. Nothing passes through from his mouth. He cannot eat. His lungs shrivel and stiffen. He needs the opium for his pain.'

'I need to forget,' Hawkstone said. 'I have pain, inside my head, and squeezing my heart.' He had never seen her clearly, there was always the murky cloud around and between them. Thoughts of Rachel had faded with other parts of his past life, caused by thinking too much on her.

'You are not old enough to forget. Do you want to talk of Rachel again? Do you want to tell me more?'

'I talked enough about her. She's dead. Her memory has to die.'

'You must stop this and get on with your business.'

'What do you know of my business?'

Mia Chang took his face in her hands. In the smoky haze, she looked child-young and small, with her black hair loose to her cute butt, and her clear unblemished face. 'You paid me for information. I have told you the information, again and again. You do not listen.'

'Tell me again about the vigilantes. Tell me about Apache Joe and his squaw, Tattoo.'

She told him of the blanket traders. But first she spoke of the three vigilantes, and their leader, Hatchett Jack Swilling, and their new scout and tracker, a Chiricahua Apache called Black Feather. Hatchett Jack had once been a stage robber of mixed success, but his woman had died of smallpox caused by a traded blanket. Hearing of the dead inside forts and burned villages,

Hatchett Jack gathered a few saloon pards from Tombstone and went on the prowl after Apache Joe – and maybe a few stagecoaches with plump strong boxes along the way. The vigilantes had tracked Apache Joe south.

For Apache Joe, what with the cavalry closing in, and now Texas Rangers coming, plus who knew how many gangs and solo men out for revenge, Mexico beckoned once again. Maybe Apache Joe and Tattoo intended to infect Geronimo. Or they moved into virgin areas of Mexico they had missed before.

Hawkstone listened to Mia's sweet girlish voice, and he asked, 'Why? Why does Apache Joe and Tattoo do this?'

Mia Chang took Hawkstone's hand. She held it against her breast. 'Apache Joe is not Indian. He is a white farmer, with a wild bushy mane of yellow hair. He rides a dun and never wears a hat. He hates all Indians for the rape, scalp and murder of his parents and his four sisters. And later, for the rape and murder of his wife – by savages. He is immune to disease. It was when he took Tattoo as his squaw that he began blanket trading.'

Hawkstone said, 'She is Choctaw and young like you. Mebbe not quite twenty.'

Mia stretched to lay beside him, her face close to his. 'Tattoo only hates the Apache. She was in love with an Apache brave and he jilted her. Men do that. They do not have to be Apache. A girl should enjoy a man for what he can give her. She should never love him.'

'Have you loved, Mia?'

'Too many times.' She pushed closer to him. 'Tattoo is also immune to the disease. She probably does not love Apache Joe, she tolerates him. He is a means to her end, which is to wipe out all Apache.'

'What does she ride?'

'An appaloosa. She carries a Navy Colt pistol, I think.'

'How do you know all this?'

She kissed his forehead and his cheek. 'Chinese are everywhere. We work the railroad tracks, restaurants, laundries, as maids and man-servants, houses like Kin Duc's, and opium dens like this one. We have farms, and stores, and we talk with each other. Information is not difficult to obtain. Most important, we listen.'

Hawkstone held the young woman close to him because she felt good to hold. No other reason. Through his murky thinking one thought stood out. One question loomed. Why was Black Feather riding with the vigilantes?

Mia Chang moved her leg over his. 'You will be a man for me now?'

'No.'

'Why not?'

'Because it's time.'

'Yes, but why not, *really*?'

'You ain't Rachel, and you remind me too much of a wisp of a girl called Little Rain.'

She hugged him close. 'Little Rain? She is the girl for Black Feather. But Black Feather rides with the vigilantes.'

'And I got to find out why.'

Mia Chang pushed away enough to study his face.

'Yes, I see you have had enough. You are beginning to come back to yourself.'

'I need a hotel room for a few days.'

'I will arrange it.'

Hawkstone frowned. 'Why would you do that?'

'Because I love you.'

'You don't love men, you said so.'

'This is true. But I will get you a hotel room.'

It took three tries for Hawkstone to sit. 'I need my gun belt, and my hat.'

'I have saved them for you. We have sold your chestnut horse to pay for your stay here and for information. Will you leave me with something of you? Will you lay with me and be a man for me?'

Hawkstone pushed himself to his feet. He wobbled and had to hold her shoulder for support. 'I leave you with a Ben Franklyn.'

She frowned looking up at him. 'What is a Ben Franklyn?'

'A saying. Words of wisdom to live by, written many, many years ago.'

Her innocent-looking Chinese face beamed at him. 'Then tell me.'

'*Good sense is a thing all need, few have, and none think they want,*' Anson Hawkstone said.

FIFTEEN

A week in the stifling room at the Orndorff Hotel was enough. If Hawkstone was to be caught in uncomfortable high temperatures, he would rather be out in desert or plain than walled in by clapboard and adobe with not enough windows, and other buildings just as high to block any breeze. Recovery from the effects of opium came faster than he realized. He still had most of his three months' army scout back pay, plus his cache of a couple thousand from past crimes. The army owed him for part of the last month of the contract. He'd lay hell trying to collect.

Some pay was used to buy a six-year-old buckskin stallion, a former cow pony that carried the name Buck. Buck had worked the old Chisolm Trail north, and proved to be obedient and gentle. He carried not one mean bone in his body. The buckskin appeared to be a mixed breed, coming from a mustang background, with the thick shoulders of a quarter-horse, but his legs were long and looked spindly, like he had some Arabian. A prairie dog or gopher hole might snap a leg like a twig.

In truth, that had not happened during the cattle drive, the long legs were sure-footed and just made Buck very fast.

Hawkstone had his Mexican saddle and tack, and his weapons. He bought four pouches of Bull Durham tobacco, some Arbuckle coffee grounds, a little salt and flour, and three bottles of whiskey. He could kill his food once he was away from town.

The middle of August, with puffed saddle bags, Anson Hawkstone rode a hot road south on Buck, with Rachel Cleary heavy on his mind. He reckoned Black Feather had left him a message, as if he knew his blood brother would eventually follow. There might be an easy trail to see, not to go after Apache Joe but to find the vigilantes, who had the best scout in the southwest territories. The vigilantes would lead Hawkstone the way to the disease-spreading renegades.

In a Tombstone saloon, Hawkstone drank 'doctored' whiskey with a man named Tom Reed, who used to ride with Hatchett Jack Swilling.

'Had to quit him,' Tom said. 'Got so he didn't just hold up coaches, he went after ore wagons, even nesters coming west. Done it on the way to tracking them disease spreaders, Apache Joe and his squaw.' Tom wore a black leather vest with a slight tear under the left arm and his tattered tan felt hat had the front brim pushed up to offer no sun protection for his brown hawkish face. 'Since there weren't enough of them so-called vigilantes to keep track of everybody – stage passengers and shotgun rider and driver – Hatchett Jack just shot them all. Killed them, even the women.' Tom pounded his glass on the bar and held up two fingers. 'Hear somebody got a wanted poster out on them. I got no part of that. I got me a wife and two little boys, working a small silver mine west of here.'

Hawkstone took a sip of the whiskey. 'Hear tell he rode south, like mebbe Apache Joe is headed back to Mexico.'

'Hatchett Jack went to a mining camp south of here folks call Bisbee, hooked up with a whore – Belle Paxton. You go on down to Bisbee, talk to Belle. She'll give you an earful.'

'I hear he's got an Apache scout.'

'Don't know nothing about that. Mebbe Belle does. You talk to her, down there in Bisbee.'

'I will. Much obliged.'

Tom squinted and looked around the saloon. 'One thing we did hear when I rode with them. We heard Apache Joe is headed way south then west. Heard he might be going after an Apache village along the coast of that Cortez sea.' Tom studied Hawkstone. 'You watch out for Hatchett Jack. He's one nasty mean *hombre.*'

'So am I,' Hawkstone said.

Belle Paxton was a lot of woman. She threatened to push her ample white flesh right out the top of her dance hall dress – the dress a bright blue, low and short, coming just above her knees. Her brown hair sprang in ringlets and fell to her shoulders. She painted her lips bright red, and her cheeks were caked in heavy, thick pink rouge. Along with two other younger, prettier girls she worked the saloon, upstairs and down. But now, standing at the bar, and looking past thirty, she had about worn out her use in any big town main street saloon. She fit right in with the Pick and Poke Saloon, Bisbee mining camp's watering hole.

She tossed down the drink Hawkstone had bought. 'Sure, I remember Hatchett Jack. He could hold his liquor downstairs and he was quick upstairs. The kind of customer a gal like me enjoys. We didn't get into more than grabs and grunts though. It ain't like we was heart lovers or nothing like that. As long as he had the price he got his whistle wet and humping done.'

Hawkstone held up two fingers to the bartender. 'You know where he went from here?'

'He went after them blanket traders. I hear down to the border, around Nogales.'

'Then Apache Joe is back in Mexico.'

The drinks came and Belle slugged hers down without pause. She looked Hawkstone up and down. Her liquid brown eyes were her most attractive feature, if he was able to tear his gaze away from the flimsy top of that blue dress. He figured if she didn't want men to look, she wouldn't dress like that, which was the same for most women. How a woman presented herself was how she was treated. Hawkstone sort of accepted a man treats a whore like a lady and a lady like a whore, except he tried to be polite and courteous to all women. They had a hard enough trail to ride in the west.

The saloon was half-filled with small-time miners, many relaxing from combing the hills and flats for silver ore. Good strikes had been made. Maybe Bisbee might actually be a town someday – like Tombstone, that grew from one rich silver strike, but wasn't an official town just yet.

Belle belched, and laughed at the gesture. After studying Hawkstone, she swept her arm down her front. 'You interested in some of this?'

'Wish I had the time, Belle. You look inviting. It's just, I got to catch up to Hatchett Jack. I'm thinking of joining him, going after Apache Joe.'

'You sure ain't no miner, you're somewhat cleaner. You look like you worked cattle some.'

'I have. Lately, I been scouting for the army.'

Belle banged her glass on the bar. 'Hatchett Jack already got hisself a scout. A good tracker, he says. An Injun, another Apache.'

'I know him.'

'That a fact? Come to think on it, he may need another rider, he's down to two. One of his boys got shot dead. Hatchett Jack says it was the Apache scout got in a tussle and gunned the man down. I don't believe it. I heard they held up a nester wagon – a young couple gonna strike it rich in silver, get their own place. When Hatchett Jack's man, Skip something-or-other, made for a feel on the young lady, her husband shot him dead with a double-barrel shotgun. 'Course, the husband had to be filled with lead and Hatchett Jack, Jimmy July, and Double Chin Bass Reeves helped themselves to the little wife anyway. I guess the Injun was off scouting someplace. I don't know how the gal ended up when they was done with her. Them three jaspers wasn't above just leaving her there on the ground. Likely, they done her a favor and shot her to join her husband. I hear there's a poster on Hatchett Jack, $1,000.'

Hawkstone dropped two silver dollars on the bar. 'I'm riding for Nogales.'

Belle Paxton pushed herself against him in a hug. 'You're ever this way again, Hawkstone, you look me up. I can put a smile on your face, mebbe make it so you ain't so serious. Thanks for the drinks.'

The border town – Nogales, spread with dirt roads, clapboard buildings, and still a few tents outside the main town, offering one dollar and two dollar pokes. More gringos lived on one side of the border, Mexicans on the other. Brisk business was done in stalls selling artifacts and leather work, mostly from smaller towns south.

Saloons and cantinas offered Hawkstone no connection to the vigilantes. He knew Black Feather would not be welcomed in town. He reckoned the vigilantes did not linger, but provisioned and moved on south. He did not want to spend the night.

At the Mexican stable he bought a strong looking mule and a pack frame. He liked mules better than horses for packing. Mules were big, strong, intelligent, and sure-footed. They handled hard desert times better than horses. He packed more flour, salt, corn and flour tortillas, extra Arbuckle coffee, and ammunition for the Colt and Winchester, four extra bottles of whiskey, and a can of kerosene to use on the dead Apache Joe and his squaw. He would be shy of civilization from now on.

After five saloon stops, where he learned nothing, he

ate a good black bean and wood-fired chicken flour tortilla meal, washed down with tequila. He rode through Mexicantown and back to the desert, the mule in tow. Many roads and trails lined in different directions. He looked for signs, some kind of direction Black Feather might leave for him. The lanterns of Nogales still flickered on the northern horizon when he watered and fed Buck and the mule, and settled down for the night.

It was not until the next day, about noon, that Hawkstone found the first sign left by Black Feather.

SIXTEEN

The signs left by Black Feather kept Hawkstone on the same trail, a trail that often showed wagon tracks, and horse prints with and without metal shoes. It did lead southwest, as if aimed toward the Gulf some called Cortez – the Sea of Cortez. He thought something was familiar about the sea, something he had heard.

The signs from Black Feather were simple. A branch torn down from a juniper, a small pile of desert pebbles arrowed to point the direction, a cactus with one arm sliced off, the prickly branch on the ground showing southwest. Many trails branched and forked on and off the one he rode. Each branch or fork he rode up to, he looked for a sign, and found one. When there was no trail, he found another sign, showing the way where he might find another trail.

The sun beat down through a pale blue sky without mercy. Umbrellas of green but browning mesquite dotted the desert around him. Ankle-high grass grew in patches, the tips already turned tan. And always there were rocks of every size and shape. Small hills with clusters of green mesquite and juniper, and other low trees he could not identify, spread before him. When he came to a clump of green growth, he searched for water. The roots had to absorb moisture from somewhere. Sometimes he found a small puddle by digging with the shovel off the mule. He made sure he had a shovel. It would be needed when he buried the charred carcasses of Apache Joe, Tattoo, and their animals. To restore some of the strength drained by heat, Hawkstone usually found some shade for a couple of hours at noon. There was not always enough shade for the horse and mule. He tried to let them drink their fill from his hat while he talked softly to them.

One week out of Nogales, Hawkstone came to low hills that rose to a mesa. There was no way around it. The sandstone and granite climbed steep as a church roof, but there were paths between them. He liked that they offered shade. Beyond them, he began to search to the side of the trail, looking for prints that might show four unshod horses in a group – a trail for Apache Joe and Tattoo and two pack horses. But too many Indians rode before or after white men and wagons.

After another five days, he came to the banks of the Rio Concepcion River. The river was wide and slow-moving, with cottonwoods and pine and sycamore to provide shade. He swam and bathed in the river and unpacked, unsaddled and wet down the horse and mule. Prints crowded the bank, of horses and boots and bare feet. He rested a full day and night in the comfort of the trees. He drank his whiskey and smoked his Bull

Durham, and visions of Rachel Cleary crowded his thinking – her strawberry-red hair on his face, her smile when
she looked at him, watching her with the Apache children. He sat on the bank and squinted at the sun
reflection winking along the water surface, and moved
within his thoughts. Evidence of other people showed
plain, but he saw no other human. Toward evening of
the second day, he shot a rabbit and roasted it on a spit
beside the river. It was not a large rabbit but with a plate
of beans and corn tortillas, it satisfied his hunger.

While he broke morning camp, he remembered
where he had heard about an Apache village south of
Puerto Peñasco. It was where the Apache, Broken Hand,
intended to settle and live his life with his white woman,
Laura Jean Dawson.

Was that where Apache Joe was headed?

Hawkstone rode on, now moving directly west. Buck
and the mule were of good nature and gave him no
grief. In two days, he reached a combination Apache-
Mexican town some called El Coyote, others Caborca.
Shacks lined both sides of a hard-dirt packed road.
Wickiups and tepees stood beyond the shacks. The men
sat in shade and either talked low to each other or stared
in silence, sombreros pulled low to hide their eyes. Each
passing horse or wagon filled the air in dirt and dust.
Though the town was not far from the river, it was hard
to know how anyone earned a living. Of course, there
was a shanty cantina, with no name and with two over-
weight soiled doves. The makeshift cottonwood plank
bar drew Hawkstone inside from the heat, with a
promise of tequila and answers to his questions. Four

101

cobbled together tables dotted the cantina floor and crowded it. Three had men sitting at them, two men each in home-built chairs.

Hawkstone stepped up to the waist-high bar and dropped a silver dollar on it. 'Tequila, *por favor.*'

The girl behind the bar did not look twenty and carried a musky sultry look with a white scoop blouse and full flowing blue skirt. She had wire earrings the size of silver dollars and flashing black eyes and coal-black flowing hair straight down to the middle of her back. She put a glass down and poured, looking straight at his face. The mahogany skin of her face, neck, and arms looked flawless, without any blemish. 'Anything else, *señor?*'

'Leave the bottle.'

A man stepped to the bar beside Hawkstone. He was dressed in peon white shirt and pants with squeaky leather huaraches, and wore a black sombrero. His blue eyes announced he was a gringo.

'Welcome, mister. My name is Juan O'Neil. This is my establishment. How may we serve you? We can offer any comfort or pleasure a man might need.' He nodded to the girl behind the bar. 'Perhaps you might like something young?'

Hawkstone looked at the girl who tossed her hair back and inhaled deeply, still looking straight at him. He turned back to Juan O'Neil who stood almost a foot shorter at his chest.

'Tracking three men. Might have an Apache scout with them.'

O'Neil nodded. 'That would be Hatchett Jack Swilling,

Jimmy July, and Double Chin Bass Reeves. Don't know the Injun. He didn't linger.'

'How far ahead are they?'

'They rode out yesterday morning. You must be Hawkstone.'

Hawkstone frowned. 'Who told you that?'

'Hatchett Jack. He said they were tracking Apache Joe.'

'He say where Joe might be?'

'About a day ahead.' O'Neil nodded to the girl behind the bar again. 'I do believe Rosie has taken a liking to you, Hawkstone.'

'Ain't interested.' Hawkstone tossed down his tequila and refilled.

O'Neil pointed to Rosie. 'Another glass, my sweet. Mind if I share your bottle, sir?'

'Do what you like. I'm done.' He glanced around the cantina. 'How do you fellas make a living?'

'We pull a little gold from the Rio Concepcion.' He poured and drank and looked up at Hawkstone. 'Hatchett Jack said you might be riding this way. He said we was to look after you.'

Hawkstone stood tall. He glanced at the faces sitting at the tables around him. He unhooked the rawhide loop off his Colt hammer. 'You supplement what you get from the river?'

O'Neil stepped back a step. 'I got three men panning for me. What do you mean?'

'Mebbe you dry-gulch strangers passing through. Mebbe Hatchett Jack gave you instructions about me.'

O'Neil blinked at him and frowned from under the

black sombrero. 'I consider that an insult, sir.'

' 'Course you do.' Hawkstone slugged down the last of his tequila. He turned and faced the room.

Two men leaned toward the table, about to push up.

Hawkstone drew his Colt. 'Any man stands, gets dropped.'

The two men sat. They understood the language.

'You have us wrong, Mr Hawkstone,' O'Neil said.

'Then you got my apology. I'll just be easing on out of town. You tell your boys to sit tight. I'll be watching that door.'

Once outside, Hawkstone mounted Buck and wrapped the rope from the mule around his saddle horn. He kept the Colt in his hand until he rode past shacks, wickiups and tepees, and away from the town. At the first outcropping of boulders fronting buttes, he eased to the left. He found a break large enough to hide the animals and tied them off. With the Colt cylinder open, he pushed a cartridge into the chamber he usually kept empty, where the hammer rested. He climbed to the top of a flattened rock and lay on his belly watching and waiting.

There would be no conversation.

Fifteen minutes later, Juan O'Neil rode a palomino with four riders behind him. They came fast until they reached the rock cropping. They slowed to a walk as O'Neil studied the rocks with a scowl. He was still too far away. Hawkstone would need five shots. No room for error. As they approached, O'Neil motioned for two of the four to slip around to the back of the bluff. All were peon dressed and had their weapons drawn. The two men hesitated. They spoke to O'Neil in Spanish.

'Do as I say,' O'Neil barked at them.

Still, they hesitated while their horses continued to walk. And continued to walk until all five were close enough.

Hawkstone rose to his knees.

Two of the men fired and chips of granite flew away near Hawkstone's boot. He kept his aim and shot Juan O'Neil through the chest. The two men who fired at him shot again, but their horses had spooked to the gunfire. Hawkstone immediately fired twice more and the men fell off their horses. Echoes of gunfire repeated around him. Empty horses ran off back to town. The two other men were about to dismount and circle behind when they were shot through the head. Three men lay still on the ground, the fourth began to crawl. O'Neil writhed and tried to sit, his weapon still in hand. Hawkstone stood, aimed, and shot O'Neil through the sombrero. That ended any movement. The fourth man slowly crawled after the spooked horses back toward town. Hawkstone ejected the spent shells. While he watched the caterpillar crawl of the man, he pulled cartridges from his belt and reloaded. He climbed down off the rock and stepped past the four dead men. The fifth man stopped crawling and turned to look up. Half his face covered in blood, it wrinkled with pain and sweated in the sun. He raised his arm and furled his brow, begging for his life.

Hawkstone shot him between the eyes.

SEVENTEEN

Anson Hawkstone rode at an easy gallop, the mule loping behind. He felt a change coming within him, an icy coldness similar to how he was in the old days, robbing and killing with no thought for victims. And the years he spent inside Yuma Prison walls. The five jaspers baking in the rocky dirt back there brought no more emotion to him than the rabbit he had shot days before. They had intended to drygulch him. Why?

Any thought Hawkstone carried about Hatchett Jack Swilling wanting him to join them dropped from his thinking. Hatchett Jack looked on the hunt for Apache Joe as secondary to his wagon and stage holdups. A threat to that kind of living was a threat to him. Maybe he figured Hawkstone was still an army scout, like some kind of semi-lawman down here to stir up his life. Or, could be he thought the scout was after him for the poster reward – scout turned bounty hunter – it had happened before. Hatchett Jack wanted revenge for the disease spread, but he also wanted an addition to his income. Likely he watched for any threat to that.

Hawkstone could not see wagons or stagecoaches along these trails, unless there was a road nearby, and some kind of wheels in and out of Puerto Peñasco.

Why was Black Feather scouting for that bunch?

The signs showing the way continued. Black Feather had to know Hawkstone was behind, coming closer. Why else would he leave signs? The trail continued west toward the Apache village south of the Puerto Peñasco. Periodically, Hawkstone let the animals rest, let them drink from his hat, and continued on at an easy gallop. It was unlikely Hatchett Jack knew Black Feather showed the way for his blood brother. What would he do if he found out?

Ahead, Hawkstone came to a small creek that eventually fed into the Rio Concepcion about a mile away. A group of green growth flanked five tepees set up next to it. The five Apache stood silent and watched Hawkstone ride in. They held Winchesters in the crook of their arm. Three women, and two boys under ten stood with them.

In Chiricahua, one man said, 'If you are Apache Joe, we will shoot you down.' The dialect was foreign but understandable.

'I am not,' Hawkstone said as he walked Buck slow. 'I seek my blood brother, Black Feather? He scouts for three hombres that might have passed. My name is Anson Hawkstone.'

'Black Feather was here. The three men were not. Step down and share what we have, Anson Hawkstone. Your blood brother said you would be coming. I am Choya Long Hair. This is my woman, Appearing Day.'

107

The others were introduced but Hawkstone immediately forgot their names. Choya Long Hair stood as tall as Hawkstone with a dark chiseled face and black hair he let hang loose to the small of his back. Appearing Day carried the look of a ten-year-old girl, except for her eyes. She said nothing. Hawkstone knew he could not linger. He would stay just long enough to be polite.

After smoked wild pig, when Hawkstone and Choya Long Hair walked alone along the banks of the creek, Hawkstone asked, 'Did Black Feather leave any word for me?'

Choya Long Hair nodded. 'We are to tell you he will see you in two days. That was yesterday. He will double back and meet you tomorrow on the trail.'

Hawkstone sighed his satisfaction. He had missed his blood brother, and now they would be together again.

But Black Feather did not show the next day, nor the day after. And no more signs along the trail showed Hawkstone the way.

The sun eased down toward purple hills, dropping temperature. Hawkstone had no idea where the cold snap came from, maybe a breeze across the cool river, or an early dip into fall. He could not ride at night, but he wanted to cover much distance during daylight. He had turned down the offer of Choya Long Hair to stay.

Beyond the tepees, when he no longer saw smoke curl from the top of the small village, he saw something in the desert – a small campfire next to a spindly tree-limb structure with a platform slightly higher than a man's head. Hawkstone had seen such structures before – an

Indian burial. Apache used many final paths to go with spirits. Fire was currently popular.

As he rode toward it he saw an Apache sitting cross-legged beside the campfire, his back to him. The fire was no bigger than a pony saddle.

'Hello, the funeral fire,' Hawkstone said as Buck walked up.

The Apache twisted to see him. 'Step down, white face. I will try not to be blinded by the glare of your blanco skin.' He spoke Chiricahua in a dialect not easy to follow – a combination of Apache and Mexican. He turned back to stare at the fire.

Hawkstone swung down. He tied the horses to a mesquite and sat across the fire. 'You are a chief,' he said.

The chief swung into speaking English. 'I used to be. Never was a big chief, no army of braves following me as young bucks traipse after Geronimo. Fifteen years an army scout. Not much of a scout neither. I never liked the army. Too many lying white eyes. Now I am headed for spirit hunting grounds.'

Hawkstone pulled the makings, offered the pouch to the chief, who took it and peeled corn shuck paper. He sat bundled in buffalo hide against the ground chill, his head feathers sparse and shredded. His face held deep cracks and folds as marked as the landscape around them. Strands of his hair the color of campfire ash dropped to his shoulder blades. His hands wrinkled like juniper bark.

They sat smoking in silence. The tepees Hawkstone had visited were a mile behind the chief. Hawkstone took back his pouch and put it in his vest pocket.

'Why here?' he asked.

Darkness now surrounded them, the only light coming fluttered from the meager campfire.

'We sit on Apache burial grounds.' He jerked his thumb over his shoulder. 'They erected their tepees too close to the bones of ancestors.'

Hawkstone scanned the black horizon. 'Seems far enough to me.'

The chief nodded. 'They will move on soon. Spirits tell me I go to the hunting grounds tomorrow. I think it will be sooner.' He looked up to the platform of the structure. 'It is fitting you speak the language of the Apache. But I talk your language better. You were sent to help me. I expected you.'

'Help you how?'

'I built a ladder. I am told I must stretch out on top and wait for the spirits to sweep me to hunting grounds.' He grimaced at Hawkstone, his wrinkles deepened. 'Those who have never done such a thing tell me this. Such words sound like the forked tongue talk of white eyes and their treaties. None of my brothers who give me this advice lay up there on a cold night to die from freezing, or suffocate when the heat returns. I will stay here by the fire. You will stay with me until it is time. We will talk in English because you are going to do this thing for me and I best be polite. When I go, you will lift me to the top. I used to scout for the whites. It is fitting a white get me started on my journey to the spirit hunting grounds.'

'You might be too heavy, Chief.'

'You will work it out.'

'And then what?'

The chief lifted a whiskey bottle. 'This is not firewater; it is a liquid that burns. You will pour it over me and the platform and light it with a flame from this fire. You will stay until I am ashes.'

Hawkstone nodded. 'Do I say any words?'

'An urge may come to you. The spirits predicted you riding here. If you feel the itch to speak, that too came from the spirits. As you can see, I believe in some spirits, less in others. Too long scouting for you white faces faded several spirits from my memory, and my favor.'

Hawkstone looked closely at the chief's face. 'You don't look ready to go.'

'I am ready. Do you have whiskey, white man?'

'I do – in my saddle-bag and in the pack.' Hawkstone pushed to his feet and retrieved one of the bottles. He returned to sit opposite the chief, opened the bottle cap and handed it to the chief.

After a long pull, the chief said, 'It is good. The spirits told me you would be a good white man. I would be sent a man, a man first, then as an afterthought the spirits told me his skin would be white. They do that, say one thing then add another.' He squinted at Hawkstone. 'They told me you would not be an Indian hater sent to scalp and mutilate me.'

'Like your brothers do to white folks?'

'Yes, but they are too many and it is necessary.'

Hawkstone took a pull on the bottle and handed it back. 'The army will eventually wipe you out.'

'Not me. I will be happy hunting with spirits. The Apache are done for anyway.'

111

A silence hung over the fire. Burning mesquite cracked on occasion. A coyote yelped from far off. Billions of stars glittered above them. The chief drank and handed the bottle back. He took a last drag from the cigarette and tossed it in the fire. In flickering flames Hawkstone saw sadness in the old dark eyes.

'Where is your family,' he asked, 'a squaw, and children? They should be here for your last day.'

'Gone. When we were young we watched you come and in our wickiups and tepees we asked how there can be so many, no end to them, we would never have enough warriors. And when you fought each other over owning blacks, there was joy in our lodges. You were killing each other. We wouldn't have to wipe you out. You would do that for us. But you didn't. And you kept coming – and taking, always taking.'

'That is the way of them,' Hawkstone said. 'They can't just use, they must own.'

The chief leaned forward. 'Yes, and you are one of them.'

'I was raised in a Chiricahua village.'

'What do you call yourself?'

'I am Anson Hawkstone. I am tracking Apache Joe.'

'Yes, he and his Choctaw squaw and their disease.'

'I will shoot them dead. Their disease took my woman. It changed me. It is making me no good.'

'And what then, Anson Hawkstone? When you are no good, what will you do when Apache Joe and his squaw are in the ground?

Hawkstone shook his head. 'I don't know. I got no idea.' He tossed the spent cigarette in the fire and took a plug on the bottle. 'Mebbe I'll go bad again.'

'No woman for you?'

'There was only one woman. She is gone now. How about you, Chief? You said your family was gone.'

'My woman treated me well. She was not just a squaw to me, my woman, none were better. As is custom, when I paid the five ponies and four pigs and seven stolen steers, I moved in with her family, her mother and father and two brothers. Her father was chief but the mother was the tribe. Women are the matriarch of all Apache. They set laws and rules and make big talk decisions. The brothers were younger than me so I taught them to hunt and how to kill the white man. Later came my three sons. Two were killed in reservation raids by yellow stripe cavalry. My youngest went to Mexico with Geronimo. Cavalry killed him at the border.' He smiled. 'But Sparkle was all a woman should be for a man – slim, and agile as a deer, she never grew fat as squaws do. It would not have mattered. I walked as a god among other men, men who looked on me with envy, who whispered to each other they wished their woman looked on them as Sparkle looked on me. I only had to reach out and she would be there. But the spirits took her first. I will always dislike them for doing that. She should be here to send me instead of you. But you are all I have. It is because I was only an ordinary chief. Not all chiefs are great warriors. Some are common and dull and dreary.' He drank from the bottle and handed it back. 'So, Anson Hawkstone, you will not find a woman? A woman is a good thing to have.'

'I got a feeling I only get one chance in this life. It was

there and I lost it. I am finished having a woman.'

The chief drained the bottle and tossed it under the platform. He reached out and pulled more mesquite to add to the fire. He grimaced, taking a breath.

'It is the same,' he said. 'That is why the spirits sent you. The Apache are finished. They fade from the landscape to oblivion, wiped out by the white man and his diseases and bullets and governments. I am finished as a chief – my life has been without glory. As an army scout I helped kill other tribes, other nations. The whites fought each other to free black slaves, yet any man born into the slavery of poverty will never be free. I have had slaves from the Cree nation and the Navajo, and yes, the Choctaw. Men have had slaves since the beginning of men, since one man walked the earth stronger than another. Slavery will always be with us. Did you fight the war of whites against whites, Anson Hawkstone?'

'I did, yep.'

'Did you own slaves?'

'Never, I was like a slave to the Apache. I was born in poverty, and captured as a boy.'

'Ah, there you have it.' He sighed. 'None of it matters to me now. I will blow to the wind as ash and maybe my spirit will reach hunting grounds. Your quest is done if you kill the disease man, Apache Joe or don't. You also will be finished with that shot. If he kills you or gives you the disease, you will be like the Apache and me – back to dirt and dust. It is all the same.'

'Mebbe what you say is true,' Hawkstone said. 'Don't know why I told you what I did about me.'

'Because you know choices of life are not always yours

114

to make. And you know I am done with all this same fool-ishness. It is finished.'

The chief sat across the fire. He continued to stare at the flame. His gnarled hands folded across his filthy buckskin-covered crossed knees. The muscles in his wrinkled face relaxed. He said nothing more.

'Are you gone, Chief?' Hawkstone asked softly.

EIGHTEEN

The chief was not as heavy as he looked. Hawkstone went around the fire. He gently laid the man on his side. He lifted an arm and pushed his shoulder under the left armpit – his knees under and the chief on his back. With a grunt, and some strain, he lifted the chief to his feet. The body draped over his right shoulder. He staggered more from the whiskey than weight. At the platform ladder he climbed up four steps that bent under the weight until the platform was even with his stomach. He laid the body down so the chief's face looked up at stars. He straightened legs and moved the arms to the sides. He climbed down.

With the kerosene or whatever was in the whiskey bottle, Hawkstone climbed back up four steps and splashed it around and over the body. He sniffled from the cold and the whiskey and the effort of his task – his eyes and nose stung with campfire smoke bite. The bottle in his hand, he stepped back down to the ground. He splashed liquid all around the platform, careful not to let any go to the campfire.

When the bottle was empty he tossed it under the platform. He pulled three burning branches from the fire and lobbed them to the top of the platform. A whoosh of flames licked up to the dark sky. He pulled two more flaming branches and poked them at the platform legs until the platform became a square of fire.

Despite the campfire heat, Hawkstone sat on the opposite side of the square fire close to the burning mesquite campfire, wallowing in past regrets over the path of his life until warmth from the fires started to diminish.

Hawkstone stayed, pulling from his second bottle of whiskey until no trace of flame remained and the collapsed platform had become gray chunks and ashes – and another bottle was empty. The sky began to lighten along the eastern horizon. He stood with Buck's reins in his hands. He took off his Stetson and looked down at smoldering ash.

'Happy hunting, Chief,' he said.

He pulled the Stetson back on, mounted Buck, and saw something to the west. A man sat his pony on the rise of a low bushy butte, still as a statue, watching him. Emerging sunlight shone off the wild mane of his yellow hair.

Apache Joe.

Hawkstone rode hard for the butte. The mule kept up, and the pack stayed together well and tight. Apache Joe had immediately disappeared. Hawkstone reached the butte and heeled Buck up, Buck climbing with effort, pulling the mule. At the top he searched along brush on the other side. Riding down into the flat, he searched the rocky ground for signs of unshod horses. He found them but they led to another creek and disappeared. Apache Joe had gone upstream or down.

At the edge of the creek Hawkstone sat deep in his saddle, squinting at the western horizon. Heavy spring rains had created many new creeks, but all would be gone by deep winter. The sun was halfway toward its zenith. Air remained chilly. It had to be late September, or even October. He swung down from the saddle and checked the cinch, and tie-downs for the pack. When satisfied, he mounted and rode directly west.

The Apache village south of Puerto Peñasco had to be warned.

Broken Hand's invitation to step down welcomed Hawkstone with courtesy and tolerance, not warmth. Laura Jean Dawson, dressed in buckskin, might easily have been taken for an Apache woman. Her transformation was complete – only sun-brown color on her face, dark hair in braids down past her shoulders – her belly was puffed with child that she pushed ahead of her with an arched back when she walked.

Hawkstone had just stepped out of the saddle when Laura Jean said, 'I'm not going back, Mr Hawkstone. Won't do you no good to say I will.'

'This ain't about you, little girl,' Hawkstone said.

Hawkstone nodded to Running Wolf, off along the sea bank, who cleaned fish with his woman while two boys under ten played around them. Next, he paid his respects to a chief so old and wrinkled he could barely walk. Members of the tribe treated their leader with reverence. Along the seashore were eight tepees and three wickiups. Poles stretched fishing nets between them. Four men sat cross-legged with Running Wolf repairing nets. Entwined juniper and cottonwood branches held dryin,g cleaned and opened fish. Three tepees had vegetable gardens. Five canoes at least fifteen feet long, built rugged and seaworthy, lined the shore. Children ran and played around the tepees. Two dogs snarled at each other. A pig snorted and rooted for food. Three goats munched vegetation that grew close to the village edge. A big Conestoga wagon sat just to the east of the village – longer than twenty-five feet with wheels to a man's shoulder. On it were three water barrels for water fetched from the nearest creek, or from a two-week round trip to the Rio Concepcion River, when creeks and smaller rivers dried. The Conestoga – likely commandeered in a raid – was necessary with its four-foot width and depth to carry those filled barrels. The wagons weighed almost 3,000 pounds empty. In addition, each family had a method for boiling sea water and letting steam run into a bottle as fresh drinking water.

Broken Hand led Hawkstone to his tepee. While Laura Jean prepared a meal, the two men sat on the ground in front of the tepee opening. Broken Hand's young smooth face looked passive, but a warmth filled his dark eyes when he looked at his white woman. Another feather had been added to his band – a seagull.

He said, 'We were told Apache Joe still rides the territories.'

'He is here and he comes to your village.' Hawkstone

tilted his hat back. 'As if he is drawn here, like this area is his destination, and has been since New Mexico Territory.' He pointed a finger at Broken Hand. 'You don't allow anyone to contact them. No trading, and keep the pair miles away. Shoot him on sight. You shoot both of them dead, and their animals, then burn and bury them. Don't let nobody touch them. Let none of the young go to trade. If you do you will all come back with the smallpox.' He nodded to Laura Jean. 'Even your woman and child. Mebbe even the typhoid fever.' He cleared his throat. 'Like my woman did.'

'We will have braves to watch.'

Hawkstone rubbed his knees. No invitation came about eating. He could not say the tribe was hostile, but he would not call them friendly. 'Have you seen Black Feather?'

Broken Hand shook his head. 'Three white men come, one very fat. They entered the village and their mean eyes swept across us. We think they look for value, something they might steal. We have no gold or treasure, or anything to interest them. We kept our rifles pointed at them. They had whiskey so our braves did not shoot them. The men looked with hunger at our girls, but they rode on. We have been watching, expecting a raid from them.'

'Black Feather was not along?'

'Why would he be?'

'They are tracking Apache Joe, like me. He scouts for them.'

Laura Jean brought two wooden plates. She handed one to Hawkstone and another to Broken Hand. She did

120

not meet the gaze from Hawkstone, but turned her eyes away. The wood plates were piled with corn and carrots and pieces of cooked fish. Chunks of corn-bread lined the edges of the plate to scoop the food. Silently, Laura Jean waddled with her big belly back to the fire. Two other women joined her as they scowled at Hawkstone. The three women squatted by the fire and talked to each other in low voices. Laura Jean was as much an Apache woman as the other two.

The men ate quickly and in silence. The food was good and Hawkstone set to with a flourish. It did not take long to clean his plate and he wanted more. He reckoned he'd better be satisfied with the one offer.

He said, 'I want to leave my mule and pack here for a spell.'

'Yes. Who do you seek besides Black Feather and Apache Joe?'

'Them same three jaspers. They got five men to dry gulch me, and they got to answer for it.'

'But they are not here. We saw them ride toward the town. When we told them about the stagecoach, they rode north.'

Hawkstone set his plate down. 'Stagecoach? What stagecoach?'

Broken Hand looked to the north. 'The coach that takes gringos and Mexicans from the border to town and back again, to the Gila River.'

'Yuma,' Hawkstone said. 'Puerto Peñasco to Yuma. Them jaspers likely plan to rob it.'

'If they have not already. It was many days ago they came through here.'

Hawkstone sucked his tongue against his teeth. He reached in his vest pocket for Bull Durham and corn husk paper. Broken Hand took his offer of the pouch, but had some bother rolling his own with his crooked hand. When they lit up and inhaled their first smoke, Hawkstone studied the three women by the campfire. They were young and looked the same, all three heavily swollen with child.

Hawkstone turned to Broken Hand. 'Mebbe they headed back this way after. They wouldn't go to Yuma after robbing the stage. Word would be out and around.' He slapped his knee. 'But where the Sam Hill is Black Feather? He stopped leaving me signs. I can't believe he went off to rob a stagecoach with them fellas.'

'A man changes,' Broken Hand said. He matched Hawkstone's stare. 'Or, a man is forced to change.'

NINETEEN

Away from the Apache village before dark, Anson Hawkstone rode Buck back to the creek where he had seen Apache Joe. Heavy spring rains had brought more water to the mighty Sanora than it had known in a decade or more. But already rivers had become creeks, and creeks small streams. Though winter nights might snap with cold, days would still be warm to hot. Sources for water already began to dry once again.

Hawkstone carried a clean change of clothes with him – shirt, canvas jeans, socks and long johns – one change on, one for washing, one clean. He set up camp and in twilight shaved his face clean and bathed in the creek while Buck watched. Since he reckoned Apache Joe would eventually visit the village, he felt no real rush pushing him. He kept the Colt within reach in case Apache Joe doubled back.

He tried to ponder a life without Rachel Cleary, but no matter how he twisted it, no living came right. All he had left he might call kin was Black Feather. Farther off might be Little Rain and the old warrior, Moving Rock.

With Hawkstone's parents dead, Apache took him

when he was ten. Except for eight years at sea and three in prison, and his short marriage in Santa Fe, he had always lived with the Apache. His seagoing shipmate, Ben Coral, was his closest friend. He had been alone those times he wandered off to track or trail, but the Apache had been his people, his home – Rachel, his woman – Black Feather, his brother. He still had Black Feather, if he could find him.

Bathed, shaved, in clean clothes, sober, clear-headed and healthy, Hawkstone, fit for civilization, rode Buck to Puerto Peñasco.

Vaqueros, impressive in tight black with most accessories silver – even the lining of their saddles – and big silver-trimmed sombreros to shadow their young faces, rode pure black or stark white stallions taught to prance in public. No ragged-clothed, unshaved – likely drunk – cow punchers were these. They looked and acted proud to be Mexican, and *vaquero*.

Not so, the town of Puerto Peñasco. A few gringo fishermen used it as a base for fishing the upper Sea of Cortez, and they called it Rocky Point. With single Gunther sail set, the fishermen sailed across Old Tampa Bay where a fish market had grown on the rocky shore. Or they sailed a little farther north into Cholla Bay and went ashore for fun and drink. The fish market established a base for a town, with a general store, stable, two cafés, two hotels, a stage stop station, and five cantinas. Stands had been erected close to the station to sell native wares when the stage came to town. Soiled doves worked the hotels and cantinas, but three small tents, no bigger

124

than cavalry bivouac quarters were south of the town entrance where a *vaquero* might find paid-for affection.

Hawkstone learned all this by observation and by drinking tequila in the first cantina he came to, called Ponchos. He wanted information about the stage robbery north on the Sonora Baja Road to Yuma, and apparently, as he found out, all the way to Los Angeles, but his Spanish was limited. Few in the cantinas spoke English, and none, Chiricahua Apache.

At the stage station, Hawkstone met Fredrico Puerto, a distinguished-looking man in his fifties who wore a gray business suit and grew bushy pewter hair with a thick mustache. His eyes were dark and piercing, under equally bushy eyebrows, and looked on Hawkstone with suspicion. He spoke English fluently.

He shuffled papers on his desk looking for the poster on Hatchett Jack Swilling. 'Ah, the vaqueros, si. Hard to believe but there are rancheros within the Sonora, three close by. It is Saturday, Mr Hawkstone, the men wear their finest clothes so they can come to town and drink and get drunk and fornicate and fight. They look much less magnificent riding home in the morning.'

Hawkstone noticed food stains on the lapel of Fredrico Puerto's suit. 'You mebbe got smallpox headed your way.'

The dark eyes looked up from the papers. 'From where?'

'Apache Joe and his squaw are trading blankets and hides. They're close.'

'I see. I will tell the *federales*. Ah, the poster.'

Hawkstone said, 'I ain't positive but I think that's the

jasper held up your stagecoach, him and his two pards,
Jimmy July and Double Chin Bass Reeves.'

Fredrico Puerto concentrated on the paper in his
hand. 'The *federale* colonel is staying at the Puerto Hotel.
I will show him this, and tell him of Apache Joe.' He
studied Hawkstone. 'They killed the driver and his
partner first. There were four passengers, two men and
two *señoritas*. The bandits killed the two men and the
oldest woman. They carried off the youngest, Señorita
Calaveras. She was seventeen, being chaperoned by the
other woman, Maria. We found the girl's ravaged body
three days' ride east from the stage. We believe they
move south after circling around the town, perhaps
going deeper into Mexico.' He paused to look out of the
window. 'I still do not understand how they knew about
the shipment. They took it all.'

'Shipment?'

'From the three *rancheros*, gold to be deposited at the
bank in Yuma. Five thousand dollars. They took the gold
and the girl, and anything of value the passengers
carried. They left the girl later, naked, by the side of the
trail, to bake in the sun. A patrol is in pursuit.' He shook
the poster. 'And her father has already led riders after
them. Nobody could stop him.'

Hawkstone rubbed his hand across his mouth. 'Likely,
they found the shipment by dumb luck. You sure they
headed south?'

'Ah, you think they will try to cross the border. You
think they ride west then north.'

'Mebbe.'

Fredrico Puerto looked from the door to Hawkstone

and back again. 'I must get this poster to the colonel. Perhaps you should come with me. Even ride along to identify the bandits.'

Hawkstone shook the man's soft hand. 'Much obliged talking. I reckon I'll be moving along.' As he stepped to the door, he already knew where the bandits were riding to. He would have to hurry. With *federale* soldiers and an angry pa on their trail, it might get crowded. Hawkstone wanted them first – and last. He wanted to know what became of Black Feather. He also needed to reach them before they got back to the small Apache village by the sea. The village carried no hard treasure for them, they had stagecoach gold. No, they did not seek tangible precious or semi-precious stones, like garnet or topaz, or possibly diamonds. They sought living treasure, precious and innocent. Having whet their appetites on the young *señorita*, they headed to the village after the girls.

The bandits did not try to hide their trail. Were they stupid enough to think there would be no pursuit? Did they think Mexico was that backward? Apparently. By the track of them, once around and south of town, they rode directly toward the seaside village. When Hawkstone caught the trail, he followed at an easy gallop. After four hours tracking, something was not right. A set of unshod hoof prints joined the three bandits from open desert. The unshod horse took the lead. Recent blood dotted sand and dirt and rocks. The three shod horses continued toward the village with some blood coming from one of them. The unshod prints followed, slower, much slower, wandering off-trail, dripping blood, the pony

127

staggering a crooked line. Hawkstone stayed with the unshod pony and its wounded rider.

Two hours later, ahead, he saw the rider – Black Feather. He heeled Buck hard to a full gallop.

Hawkstone caught up to his blood brother, and got an arm around him as he fell from the pinto. He pulled his canteen and helped Black Feather to sit next to a clump of junipers. A bullet had creased his temple. Another showed to be a back shot. The front and back of his shirt was soaked in blood. While Black Feather swallowed what little water he could, Hawkstone lifted the shirt. It did not look good. The wound was a gut shot, low, through the liver.

'My brother,' Black Feather whispered. His eyes were red.

'Try to swallow.'

'It will do no good.'

With a heritage from fierce warring ancestors, the warrior's face gritted stoic, chiseled in stone, a combination mahogany-redwood in the harsh sunlight. His dark red eyes blinked.

Hawkstone said, 'There's a village a day from here. Hang on.'

'I know the village. Broken Hand. Watch for Running Wolf. He is the reason. My brother, I will not make it to the village.'

'You got to. You just got to.' Hawkstone found himself breathing hard through his nose.

'I hit one of them.'

'I saw the blood. The fat one by the depth of the hoof prints.'

'Yes. The other two fired. I did not expect it. Was not prepared. Jimmy July back shot me. Hatchett Jack hit my gut.'

'Take another drink.'

'You need the water, Hawkstone. Do not waste it on me.' Black Feather gripped Hawkstone's shirt. 'Promise me.'

'Anything.' Hawkstone felt his voice crack. He blinked often.

'Send me to spirits the Apache way.'

'Yes.' Hawkstone's vision became blurry. His throat squeezed tight. He had to cough.

Black Feather pulled himself closer. 'Avenge me, my brother.'

The hand dropped from Hawkstone's shirt. Black Feather leaned heavily and still against his blood brother.

TWENTY

When the women in the village saw Hawkstone lead the pony with Black Feather's body across it, they began to wail. Their voices of anguish carried across the desert and over the evening placid waters of the sea. They wept until their wailing cries became ragged. The men stood and stared without expression. Even the old wrinkled chief watched from the doorway of his tepee. Running Wolf stood beside his fish nets, tall, shirtless, skinny, pitch black hair to his shoulders, no head band. The tribe barely knew Black Feather. But he had been one of them. And too many ended this way. Still, the gesture surprised Anson Hawkstone. His eyes still stung with tears of loss during the long lonely day ride. A man could not be hardened to such a display of emotion.

The three bandits had not shown themselves at the village yet. The land was flat, except for the mesa to the southeast. By now the three knew Hawkstone was on their trail, they were clearly waiting to ambush him.

Men of the village pulled the body off the pinto. Hawkstone turned to Broken Hand. Laura Jean Dawson stood beside her man.

'To the spirits in the Apache way,' Hawkstone said.

Broken Hand nodded. 'We will purify with fire.'

He watched four braves carry the body to the burial ground, the ground a small hallowed place near the sea with three platforms already raised – sent to hunting grounds without fire. He looked over the twelve to fifteen people of the tribe. His gaze rested on Running Wolf, a name his blood brother had mentioned. Why?

'Gather your girls and youngest women,' he said. 'Watch them close.'

Broken Hand turned to the tribe. He placed his hand on the back of Laura Jean's neck. 'Help them.' He moved back and studied Hawkstone's face. 'Have you seen Apache Joe? Is he near?'

'He is near. The three men you saw are back. They robbed the stagecoach. They killed everyone, but took a young *señorita* with them and left her on the side of the trail. I think they are on their way east, then north. But, first they will come here to carry off girls from your village.'

Broken Hand's young face hardened. 'They will receive a warm welcome, a burning reception with rifle bullets.'

Hawkstone stepped away from Broken Hand. He walked between tepees and wickiups to the burial ground where heavy women who knew about such things prepared Black Feather for his journey to the spirit world. From a pile of juniper and willow limbs, Running Wolf and other men erected the platform, just like the one the chief had used during the time he shared with Hawkstone. The men and women worked quiet and

Hawkstone watched.

The hollowness in his chest worked down to twist his belly with pain. His shallow breath came ragged in jerks. He began to help where he could – held limbs together while they were tied, gathered thin branches with the heavy women. Occasionally, he looked away, toward the mesa, where they waited. He wanted to get after them, shoot them down before they assaulted the village. They had to be dead before *federales* – and *vaqueros* riding for an angry father – caught them. But he felt drawn to be there when Black Feather went to hunting ground spirits. Knowing that Black Feather was the last of him, the final connection he had with the humanity of kin, clogged his throat.

And when they had the stand built and had hoisted Black Feather onto it, the tribal medicine man chanted and said his piece, then the chief spoke in a frail voice. Hawkstone stood bare-headed, hat against his belly, his head down, nothing to say. When the fire blazed, he again looked to the mesa. He put his Stetson back on. Tribal members looked on him with sympathy. A few touched his shoulder. He turned away and watched a scarlet horizon as the sun set over hills of the Baja Peninsula across the upper Sea of Cortez. A Ben Franklyn came to him. *When you are an anvil, hold you still – when you are a hammer, strike your fill.* He stood with his fists doubled at his side. They just kept pushing. They took from and pushed a man until he reached his limit and could take no more, and then pushed beyond that. Tears filled his eyes as his fists clenched so tight fingernails brought blood to his palms.

The first brave in the village was shot dead just before dawn. Two more quickly followed. The women, children and girls stirred out of tepees and moved to group along the seashore. They began to push off canoes. Two braves returned rifle fire but neither were sure where to shoot.

Hawkstone had saddled Buck. Broken Hand stood by his side, Winchester at the ready.

'Don't let your women get alone out there in canoes,' Hawkstone said. 'Those jaspers intend to wipe out the men.'

'We will attack them,' Broken Hand said. He held his rifle high. Running Wolf and four other young men joined him, their faces still sour with sleep.

'And leave your women and children defenseless?' Hawkstone mounted Buck. 'Defend the tribe, Broken Hand. If I flush them out, you can cut them down, but I don't intend to let it get that far.'

Hawkstone rode straight for a clump of growth, fifty yards out, twenty feet around, green with edges turning tan, still glistening with morning dew. That was where the rifle shots had come from. The fat one was wounded, maybe even dead by now. If so, the other two would soon join him.

At fifteen feet, Hawkstone opened fire with the Colt as Buck ran. He shot a line pattern into one end of the growth to another as he rode. The Sanora desert absorbed the sound of the shots cutting off the snaps with slight echo. He emptied the .45 and had no response. If they had been in there he would have hit one at least. He reined Buck in. While he once again looked off to the mesa, he reloaded the Colt. They shot and ran. Back to the mesa where they knew Hawkstone would come after them. They had to know he would find Black Feather. They watched the funeral fire and knew he would come. They would not take the small tribe until Hawkstone was dead. Then they could pick off the men, and when the braves were dead or wounded, help themselves to the women, and maybe carry off a couple of girls.

Hawkstone rode at an easy gallop. Before the mesa spread a cluster of craggy granite boulders with openings big enough for a man to pass through, maybe even caves. There had not been enough time for them to get high along the top of the mesa. Their three horses wandered to the east. They were hunkered in some of those cracks, rifles ready.

As he rode, something caught his eye and made him turn his head. A cloud of dirt, barely visible, rose from the ground to the northwest. It looked to be half a mile or more away. The rising sun made the cloud puff white. Either *federales* or *vaqueros*, dogging the trail – or both – not only the trail of Hatchett Jack and his two hombres, but signs of Black Feather, and of Hawkstone. Hawkstone heeled Buck to run faster. The *federales* represented Mexican authority. What concerned Hawkstone about authority was it had a way of assuming command, barking directions and orders, taking charge of any situation. As a man alone, he dictated his own destiny. He could ride to the back shooters and exchange shots and cut them down as he saw fit. Or get his fool self killed in the process. Once authority took command, his destiny would be yanked right out of his hands. And the ranch pa with his *vaqueros* would not be far behind.

The dirt cloud foretold a scene he wanted no part of. Only the trail of Hawkstone led to the village. The three hombres showed the way to the mesa.

A rifle shot snapped from the boulders. A chip of desert stones kicked up on Hawkstone's left. He rode to the right, then back to the left. There was no cover for him. While Buck continued to gallop, Hawkstone pulled the Winchester from the scabbard and squinted to see better. Sitting high in the saddle, he fired, ejected, fired, ejected, fired again and again, watching chips jerk from the rocks. Rifle cracks and the scrape of ricochet rock chips spread to the source of the rifle fire. He shot as Buck ran, to where he thought the rifle bullet had come from. There was no more return fire. With three cartridges left in the Winchester, he shoved it back in the scabbard and heeled Buck harder. He drew close to the rocks. Still nothing. When he was within twenty yards, he veered to the right and went away and around, then doubled back out of sight close to the granite. Another rifle report cracked but the shot was wild and tore through cactus branch ten feet behind him.

'Hawkstone!' a voice called from the rocks. 'Anson Hawkstone!'

Hawkstone remained on Buck and kept silent.

'I'm Hatchett Jack Swilling, Hawkstone. I know I ain't no good. I had a bad upbringing by a whore, and a

135

drunk that rolled men in alleys for their poke. I been shot at and jailed and once almost got hung. I beat on whores and violated maidens. I killed many a man, including back shooting your pard, the Apache, Black Feather. No excuses, but you can see how I come to be like I am. I got one dead man here and another wounded something awful, and a ricochet hit my arm. We're shot up pretty dreadful, and I see coming out there, running their horses almost to ground, nothing but more bad news. I'll be tossing my Remington on out, and the Winchester too. Double Chin Bass Reeves is dead. He was wounded anyways and never had much of a chance. You caught Jimmy July in the leg. All their weapons and mine will be tossed out, and we'll stumble out of this here cave. Double Chin Bass is too fat to carry. Hawkstone? You out there waiting to gun us down? We won't have no weapons. We're empty besides, out of cartridges. We used them up what with robbing stages and one thing and another. See, I'm tossing them out.'

Six-guns and rifles clattered, hitting each other as they were tossed. Since none went off, maybe most were empty. They knew which, Hawkstone didn't. Hawkstone counted three rifles and five pistols.

'See there, Hawkstone? Them's all our firepower. We got no more. You won't shoot unarmed men. You ain't rotten like us. You got a sense of fair play. Ain't that right? We're coming out, Hawkstone. We're at your mercy now. One dead, and two of us shot up wounded. Hawkstone? You still out there? Let's parlay, see how we can all come out of this alive afore that army of Mexicans gets here. They sure don't mean me no good.'

Hawkstone unhooked the rawhide loop and drew his Colt.

TWENTY-ONE

Hatchett Jack Swilling showed gloved hands first. His bloody bandana was wrapped around his left forearm. He stumbled out of the cave entrance blinking against the morning glare, trying to see Hawkstone sitting high on Buck. Jimmy July followed close behind with a bloody shirt around his right leg, wearing dirty gray long johns under. Hawkstone watched close. They stared at him furtively as if not knowing what to expect. They were a rumpled pair, looking more like they dragged along the trail instead of riding it. Their gaze never left him, eyes trail-weary, many days and nights in the saddle.

Hatchett Jack looked like his poster, a fleshy scarred face unshaven for a week, small dark eyes, bushy black brows, a brown plains hat torn and dirty. Jimmy July stood small. A little man with tiny hands and fuzz on his face. He had worm lips and long blond eyelashes and dainty movements. He had lost his hat and his corn silk hairline went to the middle of his skull. Both carried empty holsters and their eyes jerked from Hawkstone to the pile of weapons. They were pushing thirty, Hatchett

Jack the oldest.

Hawkstone moved the barrel of his Colt up and down.

The two men staggered back, farther away from the pile of rifles and pistols. Hawkstone followed with Buck taking three steps.

Hatchett Jack said, 'You ain't much for talk is you, Hawkstone? You don't use up all your kindling making a fire. Hear you shoot pretty good. Mebbe not so fast on the draw but once that hog leg is clear your bullet can drive a nail in a pine board. Now, you take Double Chin lying inside that cave, dead as a can of corned beef. He was a terrible shot. Couldn't hit the rear end of a bull with a handful of banjos. But he was so wild firing his pistol, folks just naturally ducked and run for cover.' He paused enough to wet his lips, edging a step closer to the hardware.

Hawkstone moved Buck ahead one more step. Hatchett Jack had to retreat from his gained ground. Jimmy July stood still and watched, both hands wrapped around the bleeding leg. The sun kept him from looking up at Hawkstone. He had no hat shadow protection. He moved his right hand so the fingers twitched over his empty holster.

And Hatchett Jack continued. 'I know you figure I got more wind than a bull in green corn time, but I reckon I keep on talking, I keep living. I'm trying to stay alive, Hawkstone, on account of I'm scared to death over you and what you might do. I got so much fear I'm about to wet myself. I really want to live, and I see in your eyes you ain't going to let that happen, and them damn Mexicans is coming closer and closer. You *are* going to shoot us down in cold blood, ain't you, Hawkstone? Ain't you? You sit up there like some righteous god about to give the wrath of justice, hell-bent to kill. Like you got to shoot us down on account of what we done. Just plug us through without a howdy do – us who never done you no personal harm ever, us who don't even *know* you.'

Hawkstone heard movement from inside the cave to his right. Double Chin Bass Reeves aimed his derringer out of the entrance and fired a shot. At the same time both men in front of Hawkstone dove for the weapons. Their movement spooked Buck enough for him to rear back. Hawkstone twisted to his right and swung the Colt around as the bullet seared a slice across his side with the burn of a hot poker. He grunted and slid almost back out of the saddle. But he recovered quickly, and ignoring the pain, he fired twice at the cave. Double Chin waddled out, bleeding from his forehead. The Derringer dropped and he rolled over his ample belly to his face.

Hatchett Jack had dropped to his elbows with a Remington in his hand. He aimed but Buck was in the way. Jimmy July rolled over the hardware and picked up another old Remington that he fumbled to get a grip on. Hawkstone saw him as the immediate threat and shot Jimmy July through the top of his bare head. He turned Buck enough to aim at Hatchett Jack and shot him in his left ear. He heeled Buck forward as Hatchett Jack turned over onto his back, his hand cupping his ear, his right hand empty. Hawkstone said, 'For Black Feather,' and shot him through the heart. Buck stepped over the body and Hawkstone fired his final shot into Jimmy July's chest.

The only noise came from fifteen Mexican riders closing with the mesa and the granite boulders. The *federales* had weapons drawn and clanged along with sabers and horse tack and numbers.

Hawkstone backed Buck away from the bodies. He ejected empty shells and concentrated on pulling cartridges from his belt. When he looked up, he saw Apache Joe at the top of the mesa, sitting his horse, watching the cluster of coming horsemen.

Hawkstone pointed the Colt, but did not pull the trigger. He had not yet reloaded and it was empty. Before he could drop the Colt back in the holster and pull the Winchester from its scabbard, the *federales* surrounded him, and Apache Joe had disappeared.

All Hawkstone could figure was that officers sprouted more braid then regular riders. He did not know a lieutenant from a captain from a colonel in the Mexican army. They all had ridden a long trail circled around the town and then south, and looked whipped. Always one acted in charge. He looked too old and heavy to be riding a horse. He glared at Hawkstone and without dismounting, spent some time studying the three bodies and pile of weapons.

'Aiee,' he cried. 'You should not have done this, señor. This is very bad.' He spouted a long string of words in Spanish Hawkstone did not understand, except for an occasional word. He was flushed and sweating. He looked behind his men to the north. Another cloud of dirt boiled to the sky. 'Very bad,' he said in English.

Hawkstone had holstered his loaded Colt and now fed

cartridges into the Winchester. He kept the aim down to the ground in case one of them got jumpy. Nobody took his weapons. That surprised him.

The soldiers spread out, still sitting their mounts. They too watched the crowd of approaching riders.

The officer concentrated on Hawkstone. 'I am Lieutenant Poncho Alvarez. What is your name, *señor*?'

'Hawkstone.'

His eyebrows raised, 'Ah, *si*, you spoke to the station agent.' He looked at the bodies on the ground again. His mount shook his head, uncomfortable with the deaths around him. 'You told of the wanted poster. These are the *hombres, si*? These are the vermin who robbed the stagecoach and violated the daughter of Señor Don Pedro Francisco Rodriguez Calaveras, *si*?' He stared with a frown as the riders rode in.

'They ain't nothing now,' Hawkstone said. His side was bleeding. He looked to the top of the mesa. Time was wasting.

'And where is the gold?' the lieutenant asked.

Hawkstone nodded to the cave entrance, then shrugged.

The *vaqueros* wore wide sombreros, and even weary sitting heavy-breathing horses, they still decorated themselves with silver trim. Eight of them rode in behind the army bringing much noise, and the leader among them glanced over the bodies then concentrated on Hawkstone.

The lieutenant moved his mount next to the leader. He spoke in English, maybe so Hawkstone might see the seriousness of the situation. 'Señor Calaveras, I am afraid we are too late.'

'What!' Calaveras glared at the lieutenant. He glared at Hawkstone. He rattled off a long speech in Spanish, then moved his beautiful palomino next to Buck. 'Who are you, *señor*?' He looked in his sixties, with a fine white goatee, dressed in black, a face shiny with sweat, deep dark brown eyes – a face that showed Castilian heritage – a man in charge – always.

Lieutenant Pedro Alvarez said, 'He is Hawkstone, Señor Calaveras. He identified these men as bandits who robbed the stagecoach.'

'And took my daughter.' He leaned toward Hawkstone. 'They were mine, *señor*. Mine to deal proper punishment to and to execute in a way they deserved. Why? Why would you do such a thing?'

'Personal,' Hawkstone said. 'Like you, only I got here first. But that ain't important now. They're dead and what's done is done.' He looked up at the top of the mesa. 'That's what's important.'

Calaveras frowned. 'You mean the disease spreader.'

'He's still out there. Him and his squaw, Tattoo. He stays close to the village.'

'I know why,' Don Pedro Francisco Rodriquez Calaveras said.

TWENTY-TWO

The *federales* bivouacked just outside the village, close to the clump of growth Hawkstone had fired into. Calaveras had his *vaqueros* camp farther away in the open. No burial detail was assigned to the three bodies. Calaveras intended to put them on display in open coffins leaned against the stage depot outside wall. He called it a message. The lieutenant had found the stage-coach gold and carried it with him.

Hawkstone sat on a broken sycamore trunk outside Broken Hand's tepee while Laura Jean seared the waist wound with a campfire-hot knife and bandaged it. He had a whiskey bottle from his saddle-bag to help him through the ordeal. With her in such close proximity, leaning and working near, touching him, he realized how very young she was. Her smooth tawny face looked flawless. Swollen, she carried a soft maternal glow about her, but she could not hide her youth, nor did the sweet smile she gave him as she bandaged the burned flesh. She carried her mother's heritage. If the mother looked as good as the daughter, Hawkstone could understand the preacher's fascination.

Her deep brown eyes searched his face. 'Mr Hawkstone?'

Hawkstone watched Calaveras march across desert stones to enter the village, coming toward him. That was good. Hawkstone had questions. He smiled at the pretty face in front of him. 'Laura Jean?'

'Is there a chance you might be riding back toward New Mexico Territory?'

'Yes'm, always that chance. You got a message for your pa?'

'If you happen to see him, will you tell him that I am well and happy? Will you tell him that he is about to become a grandfather? I can never go back, but. . . .'

Hawkstone smiled at her. 'But if he wanted to come here and see his grandchild, he'd be welcome.'

'Yes, sir, more'n welcome.'

'I heard his ministry is in Valencia, just off the Santa Fe Trail south of Albuquerque.'

'Yes, sir.'

'I'll make a point of stopping by.'

Laura Jean blessed him with another sweet smile and made a point of touching his arm when she left to help prepare the meal. Don Pedro Francisco Rodriquez Calaveras stomped up to Hawkstone with silver spurs jangling. Hawkstone stood so he wouldn't have to look up to the rancher. That made the man look up slightly at him.

Hawkstone said, 'You didn't finish what you was saying.'

Calaveras squinted up at Hawkstone. 'Let us walk,

Señor Hawkstone.' No mention of the waist wound or the pain searing it.

For Hawkstone, none expected.

They stepped away from the village and walked south along the shore beside the sea. Hawkstone looked off toward the mesa. He flexed slightly and jerked from the burn in his side. 'Why does Apache Joe stay in this area?'

Calaveras was silent as they walked slowly. 'She was too young, *señor*. My baby girl and they raped and mutilated her. You shot them down like you would a desert rabbit for meat.'

'Seemed like the thing to do at the time.'

'But they should have suffered, *señor*. They should have known the lasting pain of torture – what they showed my little girl. Their bodies should have been torn apart.' He walked with doubled fists. He sighed as if exasperated. 'I have two sons. They ride with me. They are older. She was the baby and they were to look after her. One of them should have been with her on that stagecoach.'

'Might be you'd only have one son now, and still no daughter. Those three were bad *hombres*. They got what they had coming.'

'But they did not suffer.'

'I ain't in the suffer business, mister. They didn't enjoy what they got. And they got it for a reason. They murdered my blood brother – back shot him. That's why I cut 'em down dead.'

'If you had only waited – a day, two more hours.'

Hawkstone stopped and turned to the rancher. 'Mister, I had enough of waiting. I intend to clean off the

146

desert of Apache Joe, and I waited long enough. I been hunting and tracking and waiting since – never you mind – I'm done with waiting.'

Calaveras tightened his lips. 'I cannot help you, Señor Hawkstone. The fat lieutenant will not help you. He must ride back to town for more tacos and beans, and tequila, and to fornicate with his fat *puta*. For me, I must return the three dead *hombres* before they stink too badly in the heat. Since I cannot torture them to pay for their deeds, I want them on display as a warning to others. Lieutenant Pedro Alvarez will use stinking bodies as an excuse not to help you with Apache Joe.'

'As you do,' Hawkstone said.

Calaveras stopped, his lips tight, his white goatee moving as his face quivered in anger. 'I can leave you two men. I cannot have anyone bringing disease back to my *ranchero*. No, I leave you no men. You killed the *banditos* on your own. You will kill Apache Joe on your own.' He jerked his head back to the village. 'Or take one of *them, señor*.'

'I just might. 'Course, Apache Joe might kill me and bring the disease into Puerto Peñasco.'

'You insult me, *señor*.'

'Yes, I do,' Hawkstone said. 'Don't none of you care about catching smallpox or the typhoid fever?'

'It cannot reach us. We will not allow them near. If you are alive or dead, that will not happen.'

'Who will go after him?'

'Another patrol from the garrison will be sent. I will see to it.'

'Sure, you will. Thing is, mister, he's here now. Once

he gets a blanket or hide into that tribe, he's liable to be gone. I got a personal reason, he gets hisself dead right here, and soon, like tomorrow. I want to know why he's here. Of all the places in Mexico he could have ridden, why did he come here? You tell me what Apache Joe wants from this village. Why does he hang close?'

They continued walking, the only sounds wavelets from the sea splashing ashore, and the rhythm of jingling spurs. Calaveras said, 'He wants the tribe wiped out, dead from the disease. He's waiting for a boy or a stupid brave to trade for blankets.'

'But he's been here too long. He knows he's got to keep moving, or somebody might just shoot him down. Or somebody *will* shoot him down. He could move on. He's destroyed many tribes in many places. He'd find more.'

'Not him, *her*, Tattoo. She was a Choctaw princess from your country, the New Mexico part.'

But Hawkstone was already back-thinking. Somebody else told him about the Choctaw princess – Black Feather. Without knowing why, he said, 'She been looking.'

'A woman scorned, *señor*. Before she covered her body in tattoos, before she joined Apache Joe to kill all Apache, she was called Looking Glass, a *señorita* in love, a young woman who gave herself to her Apache lover. You know Apache Joe is a gringo?'

'I knew.' Hawkstone had a name in his head that kept pushing to get out.

'The Apache lover enjoyed his passion,' Calaveras said. 'He was carefree and took what pleasure he wanted

148

from life. When Looking Glass became in a family way, the lover vanished. The *señorita* was heartbroken. She took to riding her pinto hard and fast. Into a draw, the pinto tumbled and she lost the child – almost her life. She met Apache Joe, a farmer who was immune to small-pox. Indians had murdered his family, then later raped and killed his wife. He vowed revenge against all Indians, not just Apache. Looking Glass found she was also immune to smallpox and typhoid. She covered her body in tattoos and called herself that – Tattoo. She went with Apache Joe to seek revenge against all Apache, but she searched for her former lover, who she intended to infect with disease. She had to find him. And now she has.'

'Running Wolf,' Hawkstone said.

TWENTY-THREE

Lieutenant Pedro Alvarez led his patrol away from the tribe at dawn. Two hours later, the rancher, Don Pedro Francisco Rodriquez Calaveras rousted his *vaqueros*, and with bodies slung over three horses, they rode north to the town of Puerto Peñasco.

Hawkstone bent as he stepped out of the old chief's tepee followed by Broken Hand. When Broken Hand had interpreted the story of Tattoo, and said what Hawkstone wanted, and why, the chief agreed and gave his permission. More important, the chief's woman – the senior of his two wives – nodded in agreement.

Running Wolf would ride with Hawkstone after Apache Joe. Broken Hand offered two more braves but was declined. The tribe needed every man for protection.

Early morning, Running Wolf looked older than his years. His face creased, bitter from not enough sleep, likely awake with worry. He was in his middle thirties but looked older. He stood outside his tepee next to a girl of

150

about seventeen. Two boys under five clung to her buck-skin skirt, dark eyes fearful.

'This is not good,' Running Wolf said. 'I have my family.'

Hawkstone eyed the appaloosa standing nearby. He harbored no feelings for the brave. He felt sympathy for the girl and the two boys. Broken Hand stood close in case there was trouble.

The girl said something in the Apache dialect Hawkstone did not understand.

Broken Hand shook his head. 'He goes with the white eyes, Hawkstone. It has been decided.'

Hawkstone looked directly into the dark eyes of Running Wolf. 'Carry enough food and water for a week. Make sure your rifle got a full load.'

The brave understood English. He understood exactly what Hawkstone meant.

Hawkstone already had the mule packed and Buck saddled. His own weapons were loaded and ready. He had two pairs of leather gloves, one on, the other shoved in his saddle-bag. He figured he would never be this way again, no matter how the hunt turned out. With a hand-shake for Broken Hand, and a kiss on the forehead of Laura Jean Dawson, he mounted Buck and waited for Running Wolf to take the lead. They walked their horses out of the village and south, the mule reins tied to Buck's saddle horn.

In the heat of midday, Running Wolf turned and said, 'I was a young brave, a buck full of juice and whiskey. She was young and pretty and wild. I did not know she was

151

with child.'

'You knew. You had to be the first she told. You seen her puffed up and mebbe not so pretty, and stopping you from hugging and playing, and you reckoned a better life lay over the hill. You drifted along the Santa Fe Trail until you run in with Broken Hand, and his band who was off to join Geronimo. Broken Hand just wanted his woman. Only, unlike you, he wanted her with him, away and gone from her Bible-thumping pa. He took his woman. You deserted yours and turned her mean.'

'I have family now.'

'You got a place to hide. You ain't hiding no more.'

'What you want me to do? Talk to her?'

'There ain't going to be no talk. We ride to them, you shoot her dead off her pony. I'll do the same to Apache Joe. No conversation.'

They rode past the cave boulders and around the mesa where short grass grew tan between clumps of green-tan growth, and the desert kicked up a sizeable wind. Mid-afternoon, the wind blew hard enough to brace against but did not sweep up dirt clouds. They were away from the sea, no water in sight. Hawkstone picked up the trail down away from the mesa, and followed it, tracking south. Hawkstone noticed Running Wolf carried no interest in tracking or the land around him. Unusual for an Apache – as if he only lived inside his head and the world outside came after.

Late afternoon, surface dirt blew like powder to partially cover horse tracks. Hawkstone figured in time the pair would circle around and back and then go straight for the small tribe. They would use baubles or shiny pieces of metal or a doll to entice children from the village, entice children too young to heed warnings about their coming. In exchange, they would give the children blankets to take home, the blankets soft, warm during chilly nights, weaved by people like their parents, the blankets saturated with killing disease.

During sunset, the track circled big around and back, headed north.

Hawkstone took the lead and picked up the pace to a loping gallop. He'd have no hesitation blasting away at them as they slept in a camp. He could not think of them without picturing Rachel Cleary, his woman, the woman they killed. He had watched the faces of the three bandits he shot down. He would watch the faces of these two. Any regrets to come over him being a cold stone killer, would come after, later, when tracking Apache Joe had become a page of history in his memory book. He had no afterwards plan. He had no idea where he would go or what he would do. He might drift north into New Mexico Territory and deliver the message from Laura Jean Dawson to her pa. Maybe, eventually, ride on to San Francisco and re-acquaint himself with clipper ships capable of crossing seas – and his friend, Captain Ben Coral.

There were the tracks of four horses, two with riders and two pack animals. He and Running Wolf rode east away from the sea, then veered north, back to the mesa – following the tracks. He carried three canteens filled with sweet water from the barrels. The *federales* and *vaqueros* drank their fill and more, yet made no effort to replenish. Nobody volunteered to make the two-week Conestoga drive to the Rio Concepcion River. Somebody from the tribe did that now.

Hawkstone was aware there might be an ambush. Running Wolf rode silent beside him, staring straight ahead, lost in his own thoughts, a man obviously not where he wanted to be. He never once looked to the ground to seek tracks. His once classic Apache features were no longer chiseled. The jowls and cheeks had softened to dough and sagged too much for a man in his thirties. His girl-woman spoiled him more than he deserved. She gave him two sons yet maintained her beauty to keep him interested.

Hawkstone neither liked nor disliked the man. The brave was not there. Hawkstone did not think of him at all. When they came on Apache Joe and Tattoo, Running Wolf would either kill or be killed. But, Hawkstone realized, Running Wolf did not make Tattoo what she was. Her reaction to his desertion made her what she was. Folks could not change what happened to them, only what they did about it. She had been young and foolish. Hooked up with Apache Joe, she was older and foolish. Apparently, Apache Joe, the farmer turned disease spreader, took much direction from Tattoo. Otherwise, they would have been deeper into Mexico.

Sunset caused the wind to diminish and brought a mid-winter chill to the air. They slowed to a walk to rest the horses.

Running Wolf broke the only sound, the creak of saddle leather, the hissing step of horse hoofs on the desert floor. 'You have decided this is my punishment.'

Hawkstone twisted in the saddle to face him. He jerked with a spasm of pain from his side. 'My only interest in you is your rifle. If you still have feelings and can't bring yourself to shoot the wild woman, you ain't got no use for me. You may just as well be dead as they will be.'

'You do not care.'

'I do not.'

'You a hard man, Hawkstone.'

'I am, and with reason. Because of you, she turned the way she did. Because of her and the gringo she latched onto, my woman is dead. You ought to be here at the finish. You, me and them ought to be here, 'cause this *will* be the finish.'

They rode in silence for a spell.

Running Wolf said, 'Tell me of your woman.'

Hawkstone locked his jaws. 'I tell you nothing. You got no right to hear nothing about her. Just aim and shoot true when the time comes. That's all anybody expects of you.'

When the Sanora grew dark, Hawkstone saw mesquite brush swept over the tracks, extending in a wide circle, hiding the trail under a black moonless night. Only the billions of stars overhead brought any glow, and not enough. He reined in and swung down from the saddle.

'What is it?' Running Wolf said.

'We'll hole up here until first light.'

'Why?'

'Have some coffee and stay awake.'

Running Wolf glanced around. 'Are they close?'

Hawkstone patted Buck's neck. 'Close enough.

They're ahead. They wiped away their tracks. Yup, they is just up ahead there somewheres around that butte, waiting to ambush us.'

TWENTY-FOUR

Anson Hawkstone saw the dirt cloud shortly after dawn the next morning. The air still had a cold snap to it with a thin membrane of dew over desert ground.

'That is them,' Running Wolf said. He untied his '73 Winchester from the appaloosa and carried it in his left hand, as they heeled the horses to a gallop.

Hawkstone expected Apache Joe and Tattoo to ride off fast. He slowed to a trot, then, as they drew within fifty yards, he eased Buck to a walk. He slid his Winchester from the scabbard. The blanket traders had their rifles at the ready, pointed to the ground.

Apache Joe's wild mane of yellow hair sprayed out around his head. He said, 'You been crawlin' my back a long piece, Hawkstone. You ain't gonna stop nothing.'

The exposed skin of the former Choctaw princess, Tattoo, looked like spilled ink of patterns and swirls. She ignored Hawkstone but stared openly at Running Wolf.

'Aiee!' she cried.

Hawkstone and Running Wolf trotted their horses closer.

Before she could raise her rifle, Running Wolf had his to his shoulder and shot Tattoo off her appaloosa. The crack of the shot carried away toward the sea. On her side on the rocky ground, she drew her legs up and tried to turn over. She looked up at Running Wolf. He ejected the spent shell and shot her again in the head.

Apache Joe raised his rifle and shot Running Wolf through the nose. Running Wolf jerked straight up and went back over the rump of his appaloosa. He landed on his neck and the back of his bleeding head. The appaloosa ran toward the village.

Hawkstone fired, worked his lever to eject the empties three times, and fired again, each bullet hitting Apache Joe in the head and chest, the staccato of sound rolling across the sky. Apache Joe jerked back and forth and slipped from the saddle, still holding the reins. He was on his knees. His mouth opened then closed like a fish. Blood coughed out between his lips. He looked up at Hawkstone then fell forward on his face. The two pack horses bolted and tried to run but they were tied together with the other horses. Apache Joe's gray yanked the reins loose. The four horses ran almost out of sight, then stopped near a cluster of mesquite.

Keeping at least twenty feet away, Hawkstone walked Buck to the bodies. He looked from one to the other, thinking only of what he had to do. He tied his bandana over his nose and mouth and pulled on his leather gloves. He worked the lever of the Winchester and shot Tattoo through the head. Swinging the rifle toward Apache Joe, he fired a bullet through the heart. Their horses jerked at the mesquite, still in sight, but then just stared at him.

Hawkstone rode Buck to the horses. They watched him, their liquid brown eyes expectant. He shot all four through the eye. They screeched and reared and bumped into each other going down. When they fell, he shot them again. His jaws were locked, his teeth tight together. He breathed slow, feeling an icy flow run through him. He had been the anvil. Then he was the hammer.

With all creatures around him dead, Hawkstone stepped down from Buck and pulled the shovel from the pack mule.

The crater took all day to dig. His side was giving him some bother when he crawled out of it. With the bandanna still over his nose and mouth, his hands felt painful and the cuts had bled partly through the gloves. Back on Buck, he pulled his lariat, worked the loop, and started with Running Wolf. He lassoed the left ankle and dragged the body to the crater and down to the bottom. He shook the lariat loose. Buck had some trouble pushing out of the crater, loose stones and dirt made for hard footing. Still keeping his distance, Hawkstone lassoed Apache Joe around the neck. He dragged the body deep into the crater. Tattoo was next. Buck pulled hard, as if pulling a steer from a mud hole, to get the four horses across from the mesquite and down into the crater, the lasso around one of their back legs.

Hawkstone threw the lasso and his gloves on top of the pile. Riding back to the tethered pack mule, he pulled the can of kerosene. He kept to the outside of the crater, dismounted, and sprinkled the liquid around the edges and as close to the center as he could reach. He threw the empty can on top.

'For Rachel Cleary,' he said in a voice that croaked.

The flame leaped and the stench kept the bandana over his nose and mouth. He sat on the ground beyond the heat of the fire, his legs crossed, and watched it burn. His mind was empty of thought. He stared at the fire while Buck and the mule stood behind him. Tears eased down his cheeks.

The fire burned deep into the night. At times, Hawkstone stood and circled the fire on foot. He sat again and stared. His head drooped and weariness made him sleep in snatches. At dawn, he pulled his spare leather gloves from Buck's saddle bag, and with the shovel began to cover the ashes. Covering the crater became more painful than the digging of it.

He spent all day at it until only a mound of desert was visible. At sunset, he placed the last of the rocks over it. Again, in the saddle, he rode Buck, pulling the mule, around the back of the mesa and set up camp. He made coffee, watered and fed the animals, and ate a little beef jerky.

He slept hard and heard nothing. He dreamed of Rachel Cleary and thought of Black Feather, and wept in his sleep.

In the morning, after coffee, Anson Hawkstone rode north toward the United States border.